The Reunion

Dream Catchers Series - Book 5

A Novel by Sandy Lo

www.sandylo.com

This book is a work of fiction. Names, characters, places, and incidents are the product of the author's imagination or are used fictitiously. Any resemblance to actual events, locales, or personas, living or dead, is coincidental.

Copyright © 2015 by Sandy Lo.

All rights reserved. No part of this book may be reproduced in any form or by any electronic or mechanical means, including information storage and retrieval systems, without permission in writing from the author, except by a reviewer who may quote brief passages in a review.

Cover art by Sandy Lo.

Published by Sandy Lo.
For more information, visit www.sandy-lo.com.
Printed in the United States of America
Second Edition: February 2023
ISBN: 9798376304396

Prologue

I lie awake, holding the small black velvet box. My boyfriend, Drew, was passed out next to me. It wasn't often he got drunk, but tonight it seemed everyone at Carney's Pub wanted to buy Drew a shot for his winning homerun. No, Drew doesn't play baseball for some bar league. He's Andrew Ashton, #12 and co-captain of the New York Yankees, my favorite baseball team since birth.

As for me, I'm not sure how I got so lucky to have his heart for over three years now. Drew brings out the best in me. He argues that fact repeatedly, though. Everyone knows me, Cami Woods, as a hard-ass bitch, who is a savvy entertainment mogul with a cold heart. Or at least they knew me as that.

Things kind of changed when my marriage to Danny DeSano, drummer for the chart-topping band Tortured, ended miserably, and I gave birth to our son, Benvenuto. That year was the best and worst for me. I fell into a deep depression that had me re-evaluating my life.

Out of nowhere, Drew Ashton swept me off my feet. What I thought was purely a physical thing with the kid, after all, he is eight years younger than me, wound up being love. Real love—not just the stuff I pretended to feel for my ex-husband.

Fast forward a few years, and here I am, the eve of my fortieth birthday trying to muster up courage to propose to the love of my life. I meant to do it at dinner, but one drink led to another, and before I knew it, we barely made it to our penthouse apartment on the Upper East Side to have sex.

Drew has made it clear to me from the beginning that if I wanted to get married, I would have to propose to him. He had proposed to his college girlfriend, Katie—his first, and only love before me. She turned him down and it crushed him. I really can't help but to hate that girl for hurting my baby that much, even though I understood her not being able to handle his career. Some girls just can't deal with all the traveling and crazy schedules, or the fame.

As for me, I would be a hypocrite if I didn't support his high-profile career. These days, my name is in the press just as much as his. Not only am I his girlfriend, but my relationship and divorce with Danny was big news a few years ago, and I am the most known music manager in the industry. I am constantly signing waivers to be involved in various reality shows—whether to be a guest judge on music competitions or to have one of our artist meetings filmed.

Drew and I deal with each other's careers just fine. We get how important it is; how our careers gave us confidence, purpose, drive and passion that we just did not have growing up. On top of Drew "getting it," I knew he'd make a great stepfather to my little Ben. The kid already idolizes Drew. So, why am I wide-awake pondering the decision to marry him? Fear. Drew's hang-up is the proposal; mine is the actual marriage. Danny and I were married for so long and we're lucky we didn't kill each other. I know Drew and I have a totally different dynamic, but still. Marriage can change everything. Why ruin a great thing?

Still, nothing would make me happier than becoming Drew's wife. Would that make him happy, though? He would love nothing more than to have a child with me.

We've been trying for months. Between my age and difficulty conceiving in the past, I didn't have to wait to hear it from the doctor to know it would be difficult, especially without fertility drugs. I decided I wouldn't put Drew through the side effects of those drugs. I heard horror stories of how women acted, and I didn't want to become a raging bitch, especially not to Drew. He still has hope though. I admire his confidence and positivity, but if we get married and can't get pregnant, will he wind up hating me?

"What's that?"

I jumped and nearly threw the ring box at the ceiling. I looked over and Drew chuckled.

"What is it?" he asked again, as I slipped my hands under the blanket, trying to casually find the ring box.

"Nothing," I glanced at him quickly.

"Nothing, huh?" he fumbled around under the blanket.

"Drew!" I yelled, trying to restrain his hands, and I felt the box slip further down the bed.

"Do you have a sex toy or something down there?" he asked, lifting the blanket, trying to peek in the dim lighting.

I laughed hysterically, "What?"

"Seriously," he stared at me.

I turned on my side and rested my head on my arm.

"Why would I need a sex toy, first of all? And if I did like that sort of thing, why would I keep it from you?"

"Maybe I just don't do it for you anymore," he smirked, tracing a finger down my cleavage.

"Um, did it seem like you didn't do it for me earlier?" I asked, scooting closer to him, feeling the ring box ricochet off my knee.

Drew smiled and leaned in closer to me. As I got lost in his kiss, I forgot all about the ring box. When we pulled apart, he held it up to me.

"What's in here that you need to hide from me?"

"Drew," I sighed, ripping the box from his hand.

"What? Did some guy give you jewelry? Should I be jealous?" he asked, not looking the least bit worried.

I'm glad he trusted me so much. It made me smile. I knew what I had to do, but more importantly, what I wanted to do. I turned on the light and sat up in the bed. Drew did the same.

"Everything okay?" he asked. "I wasn't really worried, but now you're scaring me."

I leaned over and pecked his lips.

"I love you, Drew, and I want to be with you forever, but I need to know how you'll feel if we can't have kids."

Drew's big brown eyes crinkled at the thought.

"It'll happen for us. I know it," he smiled, taking my hand.

"But if it doesn't?"

"Cami, did the doctor say something?"

"Just what she's been saying. At my age, and with my complications, it's unlikely. It was a miracle I had Ben."

Drew sighed, "Right. It was also a miracle Haley and Jordan had Aylin, remember?"

Haley and her husband Jordan are my best friends. Jordan is also Drew's older brother. Again, I admired his optimism.

"We'll keep trying," I said.

After all, trying was the easy part that didn't change anything about our dynamic other than holding out hope for something that just wouldn't happen.

"But I just... if you won't want to be with me, I'll understand..."

"Shut up," Drew groaned. "You're talking crazy. If we can't have a baby, we'll adopt or something."

I nodded, and looked down at the ring box before handing it to him.

"Open it," I smiled, tucking my hair behind my ears, and cuddling closer to him.

"It's for me?"

"Yes."

"But it's your birthday," he said, squeezing my thigh, and glancing at the time. It was 12:09 a.m. "Happy Birthday officially, baby," he kissed my cheek.

I smiled at him, "Just open it."

Drew opened the box. He looked down at the platinum band in astonishment. I got up on my knees and he looked over at me as I leaned over him.

"Will you marry me?"

His face broke out into a huge grin and he laughed.

"Hell yes!" He grabbed my face and pulled me into a kiss, causing me to fall into his chest.

He rolled me onto my back.

"Thank you," he whispered, kissing my neck. "I thought you'd never ask."

"Me neither," I laughed.

"We have to get you a ring, too," he said, rolling my nightshirt up to my navel as he began sucking on my stomach.

"I don't need a ring," I said.

"Right," he chuckled, sending goose bumps across my skin.

"Well, there is this one ring I saw when I went to pick up this one…" I laughed, setting the ring box aside.

"It's yours," he said, moving lower on my body.

I realized I could probably get him to agree to anything at that point as he loved on my body. I can't believe I'm getting married again!

Chapter One

"Cami, Matt Porter is on line one," my new assistant said, the excitement in her voice evident.

"Thanks, Jeannie," I said, rolling my eyes when she turned away.

I thought rock star groupies were bad enough. My first client was Tortured, and with me being in love with the lead singer, Jordan, in the beginning, I hated all of their female fans. And then, I decided to get involved with the band's drummer, Danny, and the line between jealous girlfriend/wife and encouraging music manager became very fine.

Now, I manage a few different pop acts, and I have decided teenyboppers are way worse than rock groupies. Grown women turn into bumbling idiots around these guys and it amuses me. But I will admit, I am a groupie when it comes to something—the Yankees. I'd known Drew Ashton since he was a kid, but when he put on those pinstripes, he became a man to me.

Don't get me wrong, with or without the baseball uniform, I'd love Drew, but whenever he's in uniform, I want to tear it off of him.

"Porter, what do you want?" I picked up the phone.

"I'm sorry, are you too busy to talk to your favorite client?" Matt asked, teasingly.

I laughed, "Is this actually a business call?"

Matt Porter is part of Sound Wave, a boy band that has defied time, and lasted over twenty years. Matt is also one of my best friends.

"Well, no. But my wife is making me call to find out if you're registered yet."

I laughed, "We just got engaged a week ago."

"I know, but you know Laura, she's excited."

"I am too," I gushed.

"I'm happy for you, Cam."

"Thanks Matty. Tell Laura as soon as I register, I'll let her know. I have to get going though. Danny should be dropping off Ben any minute."

"All right, tell Danny he's an ass and give Ben a hug for me."

"Will do," I laughed before hanging up.

My ex-husband, Danny, is one of those guys most people—correction, most women love. However, he is so hotheaded sometimes that he makes enemies easily.

"Mama!"

I whirled around in my chair to see my four-year-old son running toward me. I swooped him up into my arms.

"Benny Boy, I've missed you!" I smooched his face and he giggled.

I love my little boy's laugh. It does something inside my heart that I can't explain. I looked up at Danny and he smiled.

"Who's the new chick?" he nodded toward the reception desk.

I gave him a look of warning as I stood up with Ben in my arms.

"No way."

"Come on, don't be jealous," he smirked as his six-three frame towered over me.

"I am not jealous. I'm engaged."

"Right," he rolled his eyes. "Young Andrew couldn't even give you a ring?" he asked, grabbing my left hand.

He loved to remind me of Drew's age.

I rolled my eyes, "Can you just please be happy for me?"

"Happy for you and Drew?" he asked with a scoff.

"Mama, I miss Drew!" Ben yelled.

I could see the pain on Danny's face. In spite of myself, I felt bad for him.

"You'll see him tomorrow, Ben," I told him, before setting him down, and he took off running toward a bin of toys I kept in my office for him on days I had to take him to work with me.

"Do you know how often he talks about him?" Danny asked, letting out a sigh, once Ben was immersed in his toys.

I placed a hand on each one of Danny's biceps, turning him toward me and staring into his vulnerable blue eyes.

"Ben is your son. No one will ever replace you."

"With you or with Ben?"

I pulled my hands away from his arms and stared up at him. Danny's eyes looked even sadder. I hated when he had that sweet and sensitive look. He was so much easier to deal with when he was being a jerk.

"We've been through this, Danny. I will always love you, but we never had... we aren't right for each other. You know that."

He nodded, "It's just hard, you know? I mean, we get divorced and you're thriving. Shit, you look incredible and you're getting married..."

"What happened with you and Vanessa?" I asked, with a sigh, glancing over at Ben. "Did you cheat on her?"

Danny didn't answer the question.

"All she did was nag me."

I shook my head. "Right. Well, I'm sure you'll find a woman who's not a nag and will tolerate your temper, your drinking, and your infidelity. Maybe try an open relationship," I laughed, crossing my arms over my chest.

"Forget it, Cami," he waved me off. "I thought we were friends and you just want to kick me when I'm down. Buddy, I'm leaving, give me a hug," he called to Ben and crouched down.

Ben ran over to Danny and hugged him.

"I love you, Daddy. Thanks for the drums," he said, holding Danny tightly.

My heart melted, and once again I felt bad for my ex-husband who made his own bed and is lying in it—alone for the time being, which I'm sure will be very brief.

"D," I said, but he just waved me off and walked out the door.

Sighing, I closed the office door and looked down at my son.

"Daddy got you drums?"

"Uh huh, and he said I can bang on 'em really loud," he giggled.

I laughed, "I'm sure his neighbors will love that."

...

Around three a.m. that night, I woke up to Drew sliding into bed naked. He had been on the road for several days for the first few games of the American League Championship against the Baltimore Orioles. I was sad I didn't get to attend any of the games due to work and Ben, but I was hoping to attend some of the home games coming up if there would be more than one.

I wanted to be there for the Yankees to sweep the championship and move on to the World Series! I wasn't sure if that was possible though. I already couldn't attend the next game.

I wrapped my arms around Drew as he kissed me.

"Great game tonight," I said, nuzzling his neck.

"Sorry I woke you."

"I'm not," I said, reaching over and turning on the light.

I wanted to see Drew's gorgeous face, even though it took my eyes a moment to adjust to the light.

"Why do you have clothes on?"

I laughed as I kissed his chin and looked up at him.

"My son is in the next room."

"Benvy," Drew smiled genuinely. "I've missed him."

"He missed you too. His daddy is kind of jealous."

Drew was quiet for a moment as he lay back against the pillows and I hovered over him, wrapping an arm around his firm, bare torso.

"Will Danny ever not hate me?"

"Drew, don't let it bother you."

He looked sad and vulnerable laying there naked and contemplative.

"It does bother me. Danny used to be like a brother to me..." he sighed. "Jordan and I hung out with him all the time. Now, it's like..." he shook his head. "Forget it."

He reached out and caressed my arm as I stared at him. It wasn't like Danny and Drew were at each other's throats, but they were far from friends anymore. I felt like it was all my fault.

"I'm sorry," I sighed.

"Cami, you're not to blame," he said, warningly.

"Then whose fault is it?"

"Danny's."

I rolled my eyes and lay down in his arms. Drew had the best arms—strong, muscular, but not obnoxious like those steroid-pumped body builder types.

"Right. Danny pushed us together," I said sarcastically.

Drew chuckled, the vibration in his chest going through my body.

"No regrets, Cam. I would lose Danny's friendship again as long as it meant I get to keep you."

I bit my lip as I smiled. He looked down at me and pulled my chin up so he could look into my eyes. He loved when I was bashful; something that I wasn't often. Drew leaned down and kissed me, making my toes curl. I melted into him and my hand drifted under the blanket to his erection. Drew's lips traveled down to my neck and his hands began lifting my shirt.

...

The next morning, I could hear Ben's footsteps running down the hallway. I quickly got out of bed and slipped on my robe just in time for Ben to burst into my bedroom in his favorite *Despicable Me* pajamas.

"Drew!" Ben yelled just as I scooped him up into my arms.

"Shh, let Drew sleep," I whispered, carrying him out of the room.

"Mama," Ben pouted as I shut the door behind me. "I want to see him."

"I know, baby boy, but you know Drew works hard. He needs his sleep."

"You shouldn't keep him up screaming then," he said, as I set him down.

I was mortified, but wanted to laugh at the same time. The great thing about your boyfriend being gone for days at a time is you somehow make more time for sex when he comes home. I had no idea how to respond to my son, so I didn't.

"What do you want for breakfast?"

"Eggs Benny," he said, running down the hall toward the kitchen.

I laughed, "You know only Drew can make it the right way."

Ben couldn't pronounce "Benedict" and Drew decided to call it "Eggs Benny" and let him think it was named after him. It was pretty adorable.

"Did I hear someone order Eggs Benny?"

Drew's morning voice was deep and raspy. Ben gasped, turned around and charged back down the hallway. I peered around the corner of the kitchen in time to see my son practically disappear into my fiancé's arms. The sight of them embraced my heart.

Drew walked down the hallway, still holding Ben.

"Sorry Mama kept you up with her screaming," Ben sighed. "Girls."

Drew couldn't contain his laughter as I smacked my hand over my face.

"I know, right? Girls are so weird," Drew said to Ben before grinning at me in such a way that made his dimples more defined.

"She probably watched a scary movie before bed," Ben shrugged his shoulders.

"Yup, that was it," I quickly said. "I learned my lesson."

Drew had a stupid smirk on his face now as he tried not to laugh again and placed Ben down.

"Alright, who's hungry?" he changed the subject.

Ben and I both raised our hands and Drew smiled, clapped his hands together and headed into the kitchen. He knew his way around it much more than I did, though I did learn some things from him over the years.

"I have to get ready," I pouted.

"Tell work you're sick," Ben winked at me, a gesture his father taught him.

I put my hands on my hips and scoffed at him.

"That would be a lie, mister."

He shrugged, "You're the boss. You can't get in trouble."

"Where do you get these things from?"

"You, Mommy. Remember?"

Drew chuckled as he got the eggs out of the refrigerator along with a cylinder of biscuits to pop in the oven.

"I believe you *have* used those words."

"Ugh, I never thought he would remember them."

"Benvy, it's just you, me and Uncle Jordan today," Drew said, pointing an egg toward him.

"Yes! Just us boys!" Ben yelled.

I smiled and then wrapped my arms around Drew and kissed below his ear.

"Invite Danny."

Drew sighed, "Jordan already did. He said he was busy."

I nodded, wishing there was a way I could make things right between them. Danny was incredibly stubborn though, and I wasn't sure he could ever let something like this go. His pride was hurt, and the fact that our son loves Drew so much was just a salty reminder to the old wound.

As I was about to walk down the hallway, Drew called out to me.

"Are you coming to the game tomorrow?"

"I can't, remember?" I asked, stopping and looking at his back as he grabbed a skillet.

"No, of course I don't remember," he laughed. "I can barely keep track of my own schedule, and yours is even crazier than mine."

"That's an exaggeration," I shook my head. "The Video Music Awards are tomorrow. I have three clients performing and six of them attending."

"Oh right, Jordan did say something about Tortured closing the show. I wish I could go with you guys," he sighed.

It wasn't often that Drew showed any resentment toward his career, but in certain moments, I could tell it frustrated him. It frustrated Jordan just as much when he had to miss attending Yankees games due to his career. I truly think if Drew weren't a ball player, he'd travel on tour with Tortured. And if Jordan weren't the lead singer of Tortured, he'd travel to every away game with his brother. Their relationship was sweet, and their loyalty to one another was admirable.

I was thankful to have both of these men in my life. There were plenty of rough patches between Jordan and me, and Danny and me, but looking back, we fought like family because that's exactly what we are.

After I was finished getting ready for work, I walked back into the kitchen where Drew and Ben were finishing up breakfast.

Drew had a plate of Eggs Benedict, spinach and a biscuit set aside for me. He ran a hand over my ass, pulling me into a kiss.

"Girl, you look so good I want to sop you up with this biscuit," he said, in a silly voice as he grinned at me.

I laughed and smacked him away. Ben giggled too. I ate quickly, wishing I did have the day off to spend with my boys. After breakfast, I dressed Ben for the day as Drew showered. The doorbell rang and I hurried over to open it. As soon as I did, this puppy bounded into my apartment.

"Holy shit," I jumped as Ben cheered, totally oblivious to the slip-up of my bad language. I looked at Jordan who apologized and scooped the golden retriever into his arms. "Whose dog is this?"

"Mine," Jordan grinned, patting the dog that lapped at his chin as Ben fussed to get his hands on the puppy. "I figured she could come to the park with us."

"You got a dog?"

I was okay with dogs from a distance—grown and calm dogs that didn't drool or shed or need to be walked. This puppy with large paws, panting tongue, and seemingly unruly behavior did not appeal to me. I was somewhat surprised it appealed to Jordan.

"What's his name?" Ben asked.

"It's a girl, buddy," Jordan knelt down so Ben could pet her. "Her name is Tilly."

""That's a silly name," Ben giggled.

"Well, she is a silly dog."

"When did you get her?" I wondered.

"Last week."

"And Haley's okay with this?"

"Well, I don't think she was too keen on it considering she would get stuck taking care of her when I go on the road, but I went to that ASPCA event with Aylin, and this little pup was there and needed a good home, and A and I fell in love."

I rolled my eyes, "I would punch Drew if he adopted a dog for me to take care of."

Jordan laughed, "You pretend to be indifferent to this face, but I know you're just jealous," he said before holding Tilly's chin up to me. "Besides, Haley already went out and bought a collection of toys for Tilly. I knew she'd love her. I also offered to take Tilly on the road with us."

I gasped, "What?! Jordan, you are not bringing that mutt on the road with us."

"Watch me," he said, just stern enough to let me know he means business, but still with a small smile on his face to also let me know he didn't want it to turn into a fight.

"Mama, can we get a puppy?" Ben asked, petting Tilly who licked his cheek.

Gross! I am so going to have to disinfect my son later!

"Not unless you walk her and feed her," I said, crossing my arms over my chest and glaring at Jordan for inspiring this want for a dog in my son.

"Okay!" Ben agreed to my conditions.

"Hold it, can you go outside by yourself?"

Ben pouted, "Not yet."

"Well, until you're old enough to go outside by yourself, you can't have a dog."

Ben's pouty lips started to tremble and I knew what was about to happen. He was a perfect angel until he didn't get his way. Then, the tantrums were embarrassing at best and irritating at the very least. I was usually on the receiving end of these tantrums while everyone else always gave him his way. I am the lone bad guy to my son and it aggravates me to no end. Danny never disciplined him. Drew bargained with him in a way that left Ben content. But Mommy was the witch who always told him no, even though my dog argument was completely valid, and could be renegotiated at a later date. I'd still say no then, but he didn't know that!

"I hate you!" Ben yelled, breaking into a fit of cries.

Jordan looked surprised by the outburst and I glared at him.

"Thank you very much, Uncle J. You can deal with this, I'm going to be late," I sighed, grabbing my purse and jacket.

"Ben, calm down, you can come over and play with Tilly anytime," Jordan tried to quiet him as he placed the dog down and pulled my son onto his fur-covered knee.

"Promise?" Ben sniffled.

"Yes. Now, be nice to Mommy."

Ben furrowed his dark eyebrows over his crystal blue eyes and looked at me with a "humph".

"We'll talk more about getting a dog later, okay?" I offered. "But it's a big boy talk, so no crying, okay?"

"Okay, Mama. I don't hate you," he mumbled.

"Can I have a kiss to prove it?" I asked.

Ben slid off Jordan's knee and I knelt down to offer my cheek. He wrapped his small arms around my neck and he kissed my cheek before hugging me. Just then, I felt something slobbery on my cheek. Yuck. I turned my head and Tilly was panting as she stared at me and wagged her tail.

"She loves you too, Mama," Ben giggled.

"Great," I forced a smile and shot Jordan another aggravated look as he held in a laugh. "Tell my fiancé goodbye for me and to not get any ideas," I nodded toward Tilly.

"Have a good day, Cami," Jordan waved me off.

While riding the elevator from the penthouse down to the lobby, I wiped my cheek with a baby wipe. My phone rang as soon as the elevator doors opened. I sighed and reached into my purse for it as I heard the doorman, Gary, greet me.

I put the phone to my ear and waved to Gary as I gave my attention to the call. I knew I came off as a rich snob to most people who didn't know me, and maybe even to those who did. I didn't waste much time on chitchat and when I wasn't working, I was spending time with my son, boyfriend and close friends. My life didn't have room for much else. Besides, I was used to not letting people into my world. I was protective of those I loved and cautious of whom I let into my life.

How I ended up with Andrew Ashton who talked to strangers on the regular is kind of funny. We are definitely more opposite than alike, but I think that's why we work.

"Cami, we need to push back Rad's album."

These are the last words I wanted to hear, especially first thing in the morning. Rad Trick is a huge pop star that is one of my clients. He's made me a ton of money, but he also makes all of my employees at Out Of The

Woods Entertainment and me work frustratingly hard for it.

"Bobby, I don't get why you guys can't get it together before the new year. Rad finished recording the album months ago," I huffed as I hailed a taxi.

"The record label is laying off practically the entire publicity department and getting new people in."

I got into the taxi and recited the address of my office to the driver.

I sighed into the phone, "So? Are you hiring incompetent people who can't jump on and promote the shit out of an album?"

I heard Bobby groan and I knew ultimately this was the label's decision. I also knew if we pushed the album back, we'd be competing with Bex Moore's new album. While Rad was Bex's direct competition, he won't outsell him. As Rad's manager, I know that sounds terrible, but I'm also looking out for the best interest of everyone involved. While competing pop stars can spike up sales, it can also hurt the hype in the long run.

"Look Bobby, you'll be screwing this album over."

31

"Cami, the album is screwed if we release it in November. Publicity wise, we don't have enough time or plans. February will work better."

"Let me talk to Rad and I'll get back to you," I said hanging up abruptly.

I immediately called Rad Trick, knowing he wouldn't answer. I hung up and sent him a text reminding him about our meeting today. The entire ride to the office, I thought of marketing schemes to help amp the album up and if we could still release the album as scheduled. Suddenly, a light bulb went off just as the taxi came to a stop. I almost ran out of the cab without paying. I told the driver to keep the change before hurrying off to the building. I bypassed security and got into the crowded elevator.

I barely noticed one guy trying to talk to me with his eyes until he began actually making small talk with his mouth.

"I'm sorry, what?" I looked over at him.

Couldn't he see the brilliant idea floating above my head? I didn't have time for his useless flirting.

"Are you a model?"

I laughed as I buried my nose into the iPhone in my hand, "Yeah, a very short one."

I could see his smile from the corner of my eye.

"Well, you're beautiful."

"Thank you," I said, glancing over at him.

He was kind of cute and looked somewhat familiar. I have probably passed him before, but had no intention of getting to know him just so he could continue to shower me with uncomfortable compliments and I could shut him down with the fact that I am engaged.

"I'm Chris," he said, holding his hand out to me.

Just then, the elevator door opened and several people stepped off.

"Cami," I said, shaking his hand, but immediately pulling away, not wanting to encourage this guy dressed in an expensive suit and tie.

"Nice to meet you," he said as the elevator started moving.

"Yeah," I nodded, watching the lighted floor numbers change.

"Running late?" he laughed.

"Oh, no... just eager to work," I shrugged, realizing I sounded lame, but not really caring. I loved my job.

"That makes one of us," Chris said. "I'm guessing you're not a lawyer."

"Not quite," I laughed and just then the elevator stopped at my floor. "This is me," I said, stepping out of the elevator.

"Wait, have we met somewhere before?" he asked, holding the door, causing the rest of the elevator patrons to groan.

I rolled my eyes, "You need a new line and someone else to use it on."

Now would be a good time to have an engagement ring on, but Drew and I have been so busy that we haven't picked one out yet.

An hour later, I was trying to pull some major strings to make my plan work. I called J.J. into my office. J.J. worked for me and handled Rad's day-to-day business. I knew he was crucial to get Rad to agree to my idea. They were practically best friends.

"What's up?" J.J. asked, sitting down and folding his hands behind his head.

"The label wants to push Rad's album back to February."

"February?!"

"February 11th," I nodded.

"That's crap. Bex Moore's album comes out the same day!"

"I know. And you and I both know that Bex will get all of the T.V. spots because he has a better track record."

Rad Trick, while having just as big of a fan base as Bex Moore, was considered the bad boy of pop. He was in and out of rehab, late for appearances, and was known to throw in a random cuss word on live National television.

J.J. sighed, "Can you talk them out of the push back? I mean, we risk losing interest if we wait."

"I think we should stick with the push back and tell the fans that we're adding another song to the album—a duet."

"Duet? With who?"

I smiled widely and J.J. looked scared.

"Bex."

"What?" J.J. freaked out.

"Come on, it'll be so shocking... a duet with bad boy Rad and angelic Bex! Fans will go insane and it's a win for both artists," I said, proudly.

J.J. scratched his chin.

"So you're saying both albums will be released the same day?"

"Yes, and both albums will have the duet on it. Leading up to the release, we'll drop a single from Rad and about a week before the album comes out, we'll release the duet along with the announcement of some joint promotional tour dates."

"Cami, you are a genius," J.J. said in awe. "How did you get Bex's people to agree?"

"Well, I happen to know that Bex was trying to get his hands on a song written by Matt Porter, his own idol. Matt thought it was a little too edgy for Bex and would work better as a duet. So I pulled all the strings," I shrugged.

"Wait, so not only did you get this for Rad, you actually will be bringing in tons of writer's royalties for another client?"

"Of course," I grinned, too happy with myself.

"I think I just got a boner."

I rolled my eyes, "Disgusting."

"Seriously. Drew is a lucky guy," J.J. said.

"Out of my office, J.J.," I waved him away.

The meeting with Rad Trick went a little rocky at first. He wasn't keen on the idea of teaming up with his competition, but he liked the idea of winning over the industry. He had been warned by me that his career would downward spiral quickly if he didn't clean up his act. I basically had Rad by his pompous pop star balls, and he knew it.

Around four o'clock, I heard a commotion throughout the office. I knew that usually meant either Jordan or Sound Wave walked in. I had a fairly professional team of people working at Out Of The Woods Entertainment, however, some of the interns and my receptionist became overly excited on occasion.

I poked my head out of the office and was almost knocked down. The commotion wasn't just made over Jordan, but him, his MVP brother AKA my fiancé, my son, and the furry bulldozer named Tilly.

"Jordan!" I yelled as the dog jumped on me.

He ran into my office and grabbed Tilly by the collar.

"Down, Tilly!" He yelled.

"Two words for you," I huffed, brushing my clothes free of dog hair. "Obedience school."

"Cami, she's a baby. She'll learn."

"I doubt she'll learn from you. You don't have time to teach her."

Jordan wasn't even listening as he knelt down to play with the dog. Drew came in holding Ben and they were both covered in grass stains. I smiled as Ben was set down and ran to me. I picked him up and kissed his forehead.

"You're filthy."

"Real men get dirty," Ben grinned.

"Oh, is that what you've learned today?"

"Yup!" Ben said as Drew walked over.

He was always repeating phrases Drew taught him. It was at times adorable, and at other times, I wanted to lecture my fiancé for teaching my son things that I would eventually have to reprimand him for.

I looked up at Drew as he leaned down and kissed me.

"We were hoping you could get out early."

"Haley wants you all to come over for dinner," Jordan said from the floor where he was scratching Tilly's belly.

I looked around my desk and knew I shouldn't, but also knew I could do work later or stay late tomorrow. Now that the Rad Trick decisions have been made, there was nothing too pressing.

We left about twenty minutes later. As we got into the elevator, there was a middle-aged woman who looked at us with disdain. I couldn't blame her. My fiancé and son were messy-haired with grass-stained jeans while Jordan was carrying a little feisty beast. As we dropped another floor, a twenty-something woman got on and her eyes lit up. This wasn't uncommon for Jordan or Drew, but I don't think she even noticed them. She immediately began petting Tilly.

"So cute!" She cooed. "What's her name?"

"Tilly," Jordan said.

It must have been his voice that she recognized as her jaw dropped suddenly and she just stared at him for a few seconds.

"Oh my... wow, you're..."

"I am," he laughed, shaking her hand.

The girl couldn't seem to recover after that and it was quite awkward. I tried to hold back my laughter by burying my head into Drew's chest.

"Mama, what are you doing?" Ben asked.

The elevator reached the lobby and just as we were about to get off, Chris, the flirty lawyer was getting on. He smiled at me.

"Hi Cami," he said, but his jaw dropped once he noticed Drew with his arm around me, and then his face paled as he looked at Jordan.

Wow, even smooth Mr. Lawyer was star struck. It gets really old. Jordan and Drew didn't mind, but I knew they both appreciated normalcy and those moments were rare.

Jordan made eye contact with Chris before looking at the girl.

"It was nice meeting you," he said to her before giving Chris a nasty look as he got off the elevator.

Drew pulled me along awkwardly, taking Ben's hand with his free one. As we walked outside of the building, I curiously looked at Drew for answers. Jordan put Tilly down and held her leash as he headed to the subway station. He looked tense suddenly.

"What was that about? Do you know that guy?" I asked, trying to place where I knew him from.

I just figured he had looked familiar from seeing him around the building.

"How do you know him?" Drew turned the question on me.

"I met him in the elevator this morning. He must work for that law firm that just moved into the building."

"I bet he hit on you, right?" Jordan asked, turning to look at me.

"He was flirting," I shrugged. "But I wasn't..." I said quickly, looking up at Drew as if I were in trouble for something.

"That was Christian Eriksson," Drew said.

My eyes widened and I looked over at Jordan, now understanding the tension. Christian is Jordan and Drew's cousin who was in love with Haley and who is just an all-around asshole. He was even engaged to Tasha Torres, Haley's best friend for a bit. I hadn't hung around him all that much. I do recall him always staring at Haley, though—in that creepy, yearning kind of way.

We swiped our Metro cards and hurried onto the A train that just arrived. The subway ride to Jordan and Haley's place was kind of coldly silent, except for Ben playing with Tilly as he sat on my lap.

"Cami?"

"Yeah?" I asked, looking at Jordan.

"Don't talk to Christian, okay?"

"Okay," I nodded.

"He's just devious and I don't want him to know anything about my family."

"I understand," I said.

Drew took my hand that wasn't holding onto Ben.

"Are you going to tell Haley?" Drew asked.

"I don't know. I'm just pissed now I have to run the risk of seeing him anytime I come into my management's office," Jordan sighed.

"I'm not too happy you have to run into him now," Drew said, looking at me.

I rolled my eyes, "It's not like I'm going to become friends with him. You know I'll put him in his place."

Jordan and Drew both laughed.

"She's right, bro. Cami will completely castrate him if he tries to hit on her," Jordan said, somewhat excitedly.

Drew smiled, "That's my girl."

"Mama, are you sure we can't get a dog?" Ben asked.

I groaned and shook my head at Jordan as the train came to our stop. He just laughed as he stood up. We got to Haley and Jordan's brownstone on Riverside Drive, which they had moved into a year ago. The area suited them much more. It was quiet and scenic with Riverside Park close by. Jordan and Haley hated the snooty, rich people that sometimes can inhabit my neighborhood, and they used to live among the crowded Midtown craziness; I'm sure they have some peace of mind in the area now.

Haley came out of the kitchen and Tilly practically knocked her down just as she did me.

"Tilly," Haley laughed. "Down, girl. Down," she said, petting her.

"How mad are you about this?" I asked, taking my shoes off at the door.

Haley pushed her blonde hair behind her ears and shrugged.

"It's nice to have someone keep me company when I'm alone," she shrugged.

Jordan walked over to her and pushed her while she was still in the squatting position, and she fell over. Tilly began licking her face as Jordan taunted her.

"Please, don't sound like you're a prisoner in your big brownstone while I gallivant around the world."

Jordan just walked over her as she struggled to get off the floor.

"Mr. Sensitive," Haley laughed, pushing Tilly off her and standing up. She shoved Jordan in the back and he turned around with an easygoing smile, showing he was joking. Haley wrapped her arms around his neck and kissed his lips.

Just then, Aylin came down the stairs.

"Hey Uncle Drew, hi Aunt Cam," she said, hugging us briefly. "Hey Ben," she messed his hair. "See you guys later."

"Wait, where are you going?" Jordan asked his nineteen-year-old daughter.

"Out," she said as Tilly nuzzled her legs.

"Where?"

"Dad, I don't know. I'll be out with my friends and we're playing it by ear."

"I can't believe you're not going to spend time with your favorite uncle," Drew said, placing a hand over his heart as if he were in pain.

"Sorry, we'll have lunch soon," she said, hurrying out the door.

I plopped down on the couch and looked over at Haley and Jordan expectantly.

"We'll have lunch?" Drew laughed, sitting down next to me and placing a hand on my thigh.

"Welcome to our world," Haley shook her head. "As soon as she turned eighteen, she became too cool for any of us."

"Come on, you can't expect her to always want to be around you guys. She's a teenager and just wants to spread her wings," I said, understanding completely.

Haley let out a heavy sigh, "We don't hold the reins tight, Cami. It's not like we held her back like my parents did to me."

She walked into the kitchen and Jordan followed her. I looked at Drew.

"Well then. I wasn't trying to offend her."

Drew smiled and caressed my cheek, "I don't think you did. I think Jordan and Haley are just having a hard time facing the fact that their baby is growing up."

I looked over at Ben and put my head down on Drew's shoulder.

"And you want to have a baby knowing we'll have to let him or her go at some point..." I said, as I kept watching Ben play with Tilly, trying to imagine my life with him as a teenager.

Drew wrapped his arm around me and rubbed it.

"I know what you're trying to do."

"What?"

"Cami, stop expecting the worst."

I looked at him, "I'm not. I'm being realistic. Drew, I might never get pregnant and you have to accept that."

"I accept it, but a little bit of hope from you couldn't hurt."

"I'm going to see if Haley needs help," I said, standing up. I kissed Drew deeply. "I love you."

Drew looked at me with his deep brown eyes.

"Don't give up, Cami. Not yet."

I nodded and gave his hand a squeeze before walking into the kitchen. Jordan and Haley were practically having sex on the island in the middle of the kitchen. Haley noticed me first and immediately hopped down, straightening her shirt.

"Sorry to interrupt," I laughed.

Haley blushed, "My husband has this thing for being inappropriate."

Jordan chuckled and rubbed her shoulders, "I just know how to get her to relax."

Haley turned bright red and I found them to be somewhat sickening and adorable all at the same time.

"No need to explain. I am fully aware of the charms the men in this family have. Do you need any help?"

Jordan kissed Haley's cheek before walking out of the kitchen.

"You want to help me set the table?" Haley asked.

"Sure," I said, going to the cabinet to grab the plates. "And don't worry about Aylin. She loves you guys. You remember what it was like to be that age. You always want more freedom and to feel like you don't have to answer to anyone."

Haley smiled and nodded, "I knew this parenting thing was too easy all these years."

"Ben is going to be a terror as a teenager, I just know it. He's Danny's son," I rolled my eyes.

Haley laughed, "Yeah, he'll be a bit of a bad boy if he's anything like his dad."

"Drew wants one with me," I said, turning around.

She looked at me and smiled, "Does that surprise you?"

"No, but I don't know if I can give him one. You know how hard it was for me to have Ben."

She had a sympathetic look on her face and I knew she understood my concern.

"Drew will love you no matter what," she offered.

It was the perfect thing to say. I felt like I always say the wrong things when trying to cheer up Haley, like before in the living room, but she always knew how to make me feel better. I still don't know how I was lucky enough to have such compassionate people around me when I sometimes lacked any kind of empathy for others.

I was blessed with a beautiful family. I worried if twenty years from now, though, would I be enough to keep Drew happy? I looked at Haley and Jordan—and all the perfection that is them. I admired their love and hated it all at once. They were the only married couple I knew who had lasted this long, and looked happy, and still desired each other in such a way. I knew Drew looked up to them, and aspired to have what they have. Damn them for setting such a high expectation.

Still, they were my best friends and I am happy to have them, and so incredibly relieved that they've come to love Drew and me together. It took some getting used to for them. They seem genuinely excited for Drew and me, and I loved them even more for that.

Chapter Two

I snored so loud that I woke myself up. I heard Drew laugh and I sleepily rubbed my arms and sat up. Drew was dressed in a suit, and packing his bag to go to the stadium. He looked tired, and I felt the way he looked. It was early, and he had a long day of press interviews, and a big game ahead of him.

"Were you going to leave without saying goodbye?" I wondered.

"You were sleeping so hard. I figured you needed it," he shrugged as I crawled to the end of the bed.

"Last night was worth losing sleep," I smiled, wrapping my arms around him.

Drew kissed me softly and pressed his forehead to mine.

"It was. Your stamina is admirable," he winked.

I laughed and then pouted, "I wish you were coming with me. I like having you as my date to these awards things, even if you're a paparazzi magnet."

He rolled his eyes, "I'm sorry if my celebrity invades your life. I know how ordinary and under the radar you were before me."

He was teasing, of course. My life has never been ordinary, and it wasn't like I would ever be able to keep a low-profile giving my career and the people I surround myself with.

"It's okay, I know I'm marrying the co-captain of the Yankees. I have to accept the total package," I said, looking at him seductively as my hand traveled down to the front of his pants.

Drew let out a groan, "Don't start what we can't finish."

"We can be quick," I shrugged, leaning in and starting to kiss his neck.

Just then, Drew's phone started ringing. He pulled away from me and sighed.

"The car is waiting for me. I'm already running late," he said, apologetically.

I nodded, understandingly. Drew looked frustrated as he finished gathering his things. I got off the bed and handed him his phone.

"Thanks," he said, leaning in and kissing me.

"Good luck tonight, but I know you won't need it. I'll be checking the score and I'll try to cut out early if I can."

He smiled, but we both knew I probably wouldn't be able to get away in time. I hated I wouldn't be there if they won tonight. I wasn't hoping they would lose, but if they did then I'd be able to go to one of the games.

"When you make it into the World Series, I'm coming to every game," I told him.

He smiled and nodded, but I could tell he didn't hold stock in my offer.

"I'm sorry. Work's just crazy right now."

"It's okay. I knew what I was getting into also," he winked and kissed my cheek before hurrying out of the bedroom.

I sighed and lay my head back against the bedroom door, wishing sometimes our lives could just slow down. Just a bit; just enough so Drew and I could be in one place together longer than a few days—just enough, so we could be there for one another in our careers when it mattered most.

Ben stumbled out of his bedroom and looked over at me, pouting and rubbing his eyes.

"Where'd Drew go?"

"He had to go play baseball, baby," I explained.

"Why can't I go with him?"

"Not this time, maybe when you're older," I said. "But you get to see Grandma tonight," I offered.

Danny's mother, Leslie, was a wonderful grandmother and was always willing to babysit. She was a great surrogate mother to me, and everyone, really. She treated all of Danny's friends like they were her children. He was lucky to have her, and so were the rest of us.

"Yay!" Ben exclaimed. "Where are you going, Mama?"

"I'm going to see Daddy win an award hopefully!"

"Can I see? On TV?" Ben asked, wide-eyed.

"We'll record it and show you later. The show will be on too late."

...

The limo neared Lincoln Center where the MTV Video Music Awards were taking place; I took the opportunity to check the Yankees score on my phone one final time before facing the red carpet chaos. I was with the members of Tortured along with Sebastian's wife Tasha and Haley.

"Who's watching Ben tonight?" Darren asked.

"My mom," Danny replied, biting his nails.

I pulled his hand from his mouth.

"Are you nervous?" I asked, amused.

He shrugged, "No."

Jordan laughed, "Look, it's not the Grammys. Don't be so uptight, D."

"I'm not uptight. I just don't want to run into certain people."

"Amen," Darren agreed.

I wasn't sure who Danny was worried about running into, but he and Darren both got around in the industry. Danny was unfaithful during our marriage, but now, he was practically a slut. The two of them have hooked up with everyone from actresses, models, singers, stylists, journalists, and interns! The rest of us all kind of thought it was ridiculous, but then again, the rest of us have all found love.

Sebastian chuckled, "Stop hooking up with every hot piece of ass you meet, and these events wouldn't be so uncomfortable for you two."

Tasha smiled at her husband, "You should listen to him."

Before Tasha, Sebastian had a few hook-ups, but unlike Danny and Darren, he needed a more intimate connection with a woman to sleep with her.

"We all were not lucky enough to meet you, Tash," Danny smiled playfully.

I rolled my eyes, "Oh please, like you would be faithful to any woman."

Before Danny could come back at me, Jordan intervened.

"All right, cut it out. Let's just have a fun night."

"Aylin didn't want to come tonight?" I wondered.

Haley sighed, "She said she'd meet us here."

"I guess we'd embarrass her in this big ol' limo," Jordan rolled his eyes.

The limo came to a stop and I leaned forward.

"Okay guys, let's do this!" I said, putting my hand in the middle of everyone.

One by one, they all placed their hand on top of mine.

"So lame," Danny laughed as he was the last one to put his hand in the circle.

"Sound Wave does it no problem," I smirked at him.

"That's because they *are* lame," Danny said.

I stuck out my tongue and we broke our hands away just as the limo door opened. Tortured's publicist met us on the red carpet and escorted us through to the reporters. I stayed back as Tortured did interviews. Haley and Tasha hung back with me most of the time, but were called over once in a while for photos with the guys. I am glad I am no longer a musician's wife. I hated posing for the press and plastering on a phony smile for some story they'd most likely twist. Sure, I still dealt with it when I was with Drew, but we didn't get to go to as many public functions together due to our crazy schedules.

Most of the night I mingled with people on the red carpet. There were publicists, managers, and celebrities I have worked with over the years. Haley's friend Meghan, a popular fashion designer, along with Chloe, Tortured's stylist, came over to chat with us for a bit. Chloe had dated Darren briefly, and she practically ran away before he spotted her. I don't know what that guy does to make women hate him by the end of every fling!

My other clients were in close vicinity so I could keep an eye on things, even though I knew Colin, Lisa Ann and J.J. could handle it, along with some of the publicists that were on hand. Though J.J. was standing around, alternating between looking at his phone and the red carpet entrance as if he were waiting on someone. I walked over to him.

"Hey, where's Rad?"

"He said he was waiting on his date," he sighed.

"His date? J.J., you should be with him. He needs to be front and center tonight if we want to salvage what's left of his image. I want him schmoozing with every reporter," I warned him. "Get him here now."

He nodded, and began punching away at his phone. I turned around just in time to hear the screams. Relief washed over me as Rad Trick came into view. He was wearing a red and black suit, which I thought looked great on him. He offered his arm to a girl and she had on a purple dress that looked like something Haley had worn years ago. My mouth dropped as I saw the girl's face.

I went into shock. Aylin Ashton, *our Aylin*, on the arm of bad boy Rad Trick? No way are her parents going to be happy about it. No way am I happy about it! Not only was Rad five years older than Aylin, but he had a drug problem, picked fights in bars, and it was not uncommon to find more than one girl in his hotel room at any given time. If Jordan didn't kill Rad, I'm pretty sure I would!

As Rad signed autographs, just like I had advised him in our meeting, I took the opportunity to approach Aylin, who photographers seemed to want to get pictures of. I'm not sure if they wanted shots of her because she was Rad's date or Jordan's daughter, or because she simply was stunning, but I wanted to protect her from it all. I loved this kid like family and damned if I wanted her sucked into my loser client's drama.

"A, what are you doing?" I asked immediately.

"I'm being supportive," she said, looking at me weirdly.

"Of who? You should be by your dad's side."

"Aunt Cam, really? I can't be Rad's date because my dad is up against him for an award?"

"No, you can't be Rad's date because he has a lot of issues," I gritted my teeth.

She rolled her eyes, "Everyone has issues, and people change."

"Is this your mom's dress?"

"Yeah, it's a vintage Meghan Williams design now," she said with a smile.

This was the dress that practically put Meghan on the map. She designed it and gave it to Haley to wear on her first date with Jordan. Haley bragged about it to a bunch of socialites, hoping to get Meghan an in, and it worked!

Rad walked over to us and put his arm around Aylin.

"Oh right, you two know each other," he smirked.

I wanted to slap his sneaky smirk away and rip off his black polished nails one by one as they caressed Aylin's bare shoulder. I was steaming. I have dealt with a ton of crap representing this ass, and this is how he repays me? Jordan was going to fly off the handle—in public—at a televised event!

"When did this start?" I wondered.

Rad shrugged, probably not recalling.

"Remember when I babysat Ben for you a few weeks ago and I came to drop him off at the office?" Aylin asked. "I ran into Rad and we went for a walk in Bryant Park and..."

"I don't have time for this," I cut her off, really not wanting to hear the details.

Aylin looked pissed at me, but I wasn't too thrilled with her choices tonight.

"Rad, J.J. is waiting for you. Aylin, all I have to say is good luck with your parents," I huffed before walking away.

"I'm nineteen," I heard her call out as I walked away.

Nineteen, that's just a number. At nineteen, I was out on my own. I was hungry for opportunity. I fell in love with Jordan, who didn't feel the same way as I did, and I hurt so bad that I dove into a frustrating relationship with Danny, a bad boy himself. I know nineteen seems old enough, but you're never old enough to survive heartbreak, especially your first one. I wish I could explain all of that to her. She was always a smart girl, but intelligence flies out the window in relationships. I don't know if she gets that. Her parents never taught her that. They were bound perfectly together and by her wanting to wear the dress her mother wore for her first date with her father just makes it clear that she thinks their story could be her story...*with Rad.*

Maybe I'm misjudging the guy, but I've known him a lot longer than Aylin has. I've heard the false promises and the proclamations of love when it was really lust all because you lie to yourself that what you have is different.

I want better for Aylin than some on-and-off-the-wagon pop star that would be—sorry to say it—washed up in five years. He was my client and making plenty of money, but I knew an act like him had an expiration date. His wild behavior was just shortening his career more.

I yearned for Drew as I headed back over to Tortured, wondering if Aylin had been spotted yet. I wanted Drew to remind me that he was *my* real love story. That my broken heart led me to him; to show Aylin he was the type of man you give your heart to;

not the bad boys, but the guys who have big hearts as well as passion.

I immediately approached Haley while Jordan was speaking to a television camera.

"Cami, what's wrong?" She asked.

"Aylin is here," I sighed.

"Where?" She said and I pointed her out.

Aylin was posing with Rad as photographers snapped photos nonstop. She rarely liked that sort of thing. Jordan usually refused for her and Haley to be photographed most of the time. He wanted to protect them from the limelight as much as possible.

Haley's eyes went wide.

"What is she doing?! And in my dress?"

"You have to help calm Jordan down. If there is any kind of hostility between him and Rad, it will wind up as a headline...and I don't know if that's the type of publicity either of my clients need right now."

Or maybe I was going soft? Back in the day, I was the one jumping into arguments and fights. I would attack anyone who was out to hurt the people I cared about or me.

Or maybe I just knew whatever Jordan did, it would just wind up hurting Aylin in the end. It's unfortunate that parents really just want to protect their kids, but in doing so, sometimes they push them further away. Or teach them to be afraid or not to trust. We're all guilty of either causing or feeling these emotions, and I didn't want Jordan and Haley to push that on Aylin right now. She was still so untainted and full of hope.

Just then, Tortured's publicist, Melissa stepped over.

"This is great," she clapped her hands together.

"What's great?"

"We'll get a picture of Jordan with Rad and Aylin. It'll be top news tomorrow!" she squeaked.

"Mel," I sighed. "Jordan is likely to knock Rad out if he gets near him."

"Oh come on, so Aylin is Rad's date. Jordan can take it. Besides, if he does knock him out, still a publicity gold mine," she winked at Haley and me.

Haley groaned, "I'll go tell him to smile pretty while that punk has his arm around our daughter."

I watched Haley walk over to Jordan and the usual ease in his face disappeared as she spoke to him. His eyes searched for Aylin and Rad as they walked toward us. I then looked at Melissa, who was directing some photographers toward them. Jordan shook Rad's hand, and I'm pretty sure he was trying to break it before he kissed Aylin's cheek, all as the photographers captured the moment. They all posed for a group photo and once the photographers had dispersed, Jordan looked at Aylin while Rad was pulled away by J.J. for interviews.

"Are you sitting with us?"

"Dad, I'm Rad's date," Aylin said apologetically.

"A, I'm not trying to be an overbearing father, but why Rad Trick?"

She shrugged, "We're just friends. He's kind of sweet underneath it all."

Haley took Jordan's hand and squeezed, "We trust your judgment."

I could tell Jordan didn't quite feel the same as his wife at that moment. I know Haley was putting herself in her daughter's shoes. It wasn't like her parents had approved of Jordan at first.

Aylin sighed, "I hope so. I'm not stupid. I know Rad's image. But it's an image, that's all."

This is where I wanted to butt in. Yes, there were plenty of fake images in the entertainment industry, but Rad Trick's tarnished image was the reality. I just hoped Aylin was being honest about just being friends with him.

"Guys, we have to go inside," I interrupted.

"Maybe you'll come sit with us when Rad performs?" I asked Aylin, rubbing her shoulder.

She nodded.

"You look just like your mom tonight," Jordan told her and kissed her cheek.

"Thanks Dad," she said. "Don't worry, okay? I'll be going home with you guys tonight."

"You better," he winked.

We walked inside Lincoln Center and were shown to our seats. I sat next to Danny and looked at my phone. The Yankee game was going into extra innings. Danny peered over at the screen.

"It's hard not having a date to these things," he sighed.

I rolled my eyes, "You bring dates all the time. You couldn't get one of your underwear model friends or twenty-something pop singers to come with you?"

"I could have, but I figured since you were coming alone..." he shrugged.

"You figured what?" I scoffed. "That we could pretend?"

"No," he sucked his teeth. "I meant... I didn't want you to feel uncomfortable."

"You're making me feel uncomfortable right now," I told him.

"I just—it's nice to be with you without having to worry about some chick on my arm or to have to avoid you and Drew."

"Danny, maybe you shouldn't avoid us," I sighed. "Drew wants to be your friend still."

"That's not going to happen."

"Well, then stop being weird, okay?" I asked. "All you do is mope about not having anyone and when you do have someone, you're not happy with her. I don't remember you being this whiny when we were married," I rolled my eyes.

"Yeah, well, I don't remember you being nice when we were married," he shot at me.

I laughed, "Okay, I was a bitch to you and still am. You bring it out most in me."

"Guys," Darren looked over at us. "Don't fight."

"We're just being normal," Danny shrugged.

"Yeah, I know," Darren shook his head.

Danny and I had to laugh. We would always bicker; it was just how we were together.

The awards show began with a not so funny comedian making somewhat offensive jokes. He made fun of Sound Wave's age and Rad's drug problem before making homosexual remarks about Bex Moore. At least he didn't pick on Tortured... yet.

"Is that Danny D. from Tortured?" The host called out, pretending to look for Danny. "Wait, does your date actually have clothes on?"

I wanted to disappear since I knew the camera would flash to us.

"Oh, that's not your date... that's the Yankees' ball girl."

The crowd oohed at the sexual undertone to the joke. I wanted to punch the host out, but so did Danny apparently, who stood up and began shouting profanities. I grabbed his arm, trying to pull him back down.

Luckily, the first presenter was announced. Danny sat back down and was flushed.

"Calm down," I said.

"Look, I don't care that he messes with me, but..."

"He actually said it to mess with you, not me," I sighed. "It's no secret about our past."

"It was a douche thing to say," Danny huffed.

"Yes, and that's what he's getting paid for. That was actually the funniest thing he said all night unfortunately," I rolled my eyes.

"You okay?" I heard Haley call.

"Fine," I waved her off.

I took my phone out to text Drew about my night so far. I pretty much was trying to extinguish fights and was humiliated by a former *Saturday Night Live* alumnus. Oh, the glamourous life I lead!

I knew Drew wouldn't reply; not until the seventh inning stretch—and it was only the fourth inning. The Yanks were up by one already, and I couldn't help but be distracted by keeping tabs on the game while the show was going on. An hour later, I was surprised I didn't hear from Drew. It was the top of the eighth and the Yankees were still in the lead. I smiled before looking for the most updated commentary of the game on Twitter. The first headline that I read had me shouting in the middle of Topaz—a pop singer and acquaintance of Drew's—acceptance speech.

A few people looked at me, but I didn't care as I opened the link to the article titled, "Yankees About To Head To The World Series While Ashton Rushed to the E.R.". I skimmed through the article to find out Drew collided with a runner and possibly dislocated his shoulder. I immediately hopped up and received curious looks.

"Cam, what's going on?" Danny asked, as I practically tripped into Darren's lap.

"Are you okay?" Sebastian asked as I passed him.

"I have to go, I'm sorry," I sighed. "Drew's in the hospital."

"What happened?" Jordan asked, bolting up.

"He was injured during the game."

"I'm coming too."

"No, you can't," I told him, though I wanted him to come with me. "You have to perform, remember?"

Jordan sighed and wanted to object.

"How bad is it?"

"I'm not sure—a dislocated shoulder at the most," I offered.

I could see the struggle in his face. He wanted to be at the hospital for his brother. Drew was more important to him than performing for millions of people watching on T.V. Jordan also knew I had enough worry coursing through me over Drew than to have to smooth over burned bridges with MTV tomorrow when Tortured cancelled their performance.

"Tell Drew I'll be there right after the show," Jordan said. "Hale, why don't you go with Cami?"

Haley nodded, "Of course. Good luck, baby. Don't worry."

She kissed Jordan before following behind me. I found a bodyguard for Rad Trick that I knew well.

"Fred, we need a car to take us to NYU Hospital. My boyfriend is in the E.R.," I explained.

"I got you, Miss Cami," he said, jogging outside.

"You don't have to come, Haley. Drew will understand if you come later with Jordan."

Haley shook her head in disagreement.

"I know that. I'm coming to be there for you," she said, and I smiled gratefully.

Fred came back in and waved us out of the building. We got into a black Mercedes with tinted windows. I told the driver where to go while I tried to find out what room Drew was in and what I should expect.

I couldn't get in touch with Drew at all. I called one of his best friends and teammates, Cisco Rodriguez. Drew and Cisco were co-captains of the team.

"Hey Cami," Cisco answered. "I guess you heard?"

"Yeah, I'm on my way to the hospital. How bad is it?"

"I'm not sure. It looked pretty bad. He was in a lot of pain."

I felt tears come to my eyes at the mere thought of my man in any kind of pain. I asked Cisco the room number and told him I'd get there as soon as possible. I hung up the phone and felt Haley's hand on the back of my hand, squeezing it reassuringly.

"Look, worst case scenario is he'll have some months of rehab, right?" Haley asked.

I sighed, "Drew won't get to play in the World Series. He's probably more upset by that than the physical pain."

Drew was one of those players that still had such a love of the game. It was incredibly hard to not be there for him. I should have been there with him, watching his moments of glory as he brought his team closer to the World Series. Instead, I was wrangling a bunch of grown men at an awards show. I didn't need to be at Lincoln Center; my clients had Colin, Lisa Ann, and J.J., on top of publicists to keep them in line. I was just a control freak, and I wanted to be there, showing my pride for what my artists have contributed to music this year. It was my pride and need for control that made me miss Drew's win, and to not be there for him when he got hurt.

We made it to the hospital and Cisco directed us to the room Drew was moved to. He was lying in the bed, his right arm in a sling and a few scratches on that side of his face as well.

"Hey," Drew forced a smile at me as we walked in.

I hurried over to the bed and ran my fingers through his hair.

"You look hot," he said, reaching over and taking my hand into his left one, his eyes glancing over my mini-dress.

I wiped my tears and laughed, "Thanks."

"Aw, you were worried about me?" he smirked, looking sexy, even all scratched up.

I sat down on his bed and kissed him.

"Still a flirt, even in a hospital bed."

Haley walked closer, "It's a good thing you're a lefty, huh?"

Drew and I both stared at her, our minds both going into the gutter and not thinking of baseball at all. Haley caught on a moment later.

"Ugh, I meant so you can still do day-to-day things, like write, and eat, and throw a baseball!" She practically hissed.

Drew chuckled and I couldn't help but laugh.

"Yeah," Drew nodded. "It's a good thing I'm a lefty," he winked at me, and I smiled at him.

"So, what did the doctor say?" Haley asked, changing the subject.

"My shoulder is dislocated and it could be up to twelve weeks to fully recover. There goes the World Series for me."

"You'll be back for spring training, though," I offered.

Drew shrugged, "Yeah."

"You'll be good as new," Haley told him, sensing worry.

We're not used to Drew being worried or negative in any sort of way.

"Do you mind if I talk to Cami alone for a few minutes?"

"Of course not," Haley said with a smile before walking out of the room.

Drew looked at me and I leaned over to kiss him again.

"Are you in a lot of pain?"

He shrugged, "A little. The pain killers are starting to work."

I nodded, "I'm really sorry."

"For what?"

"For you getting hurt. For me not being here," I said, looking at him.

"Stop looking at me with those guilty, beautiful blue eyes," he said. "I think me getting hurt was a message."

I looked at him funny, "What kind of message? Like from God?"

"Maybe. You know, we're getting married and trying to start a family... I've always been prepared to retire when that happened..."

Wow. I didn't know what to say to that. Drew had said he used to dream of retiring early to start a family, but that was before we were serious, and before I knew I would be the woman he would retire for.

"Drew, you're loopy from the meds," I laughed him off.

"That's beside the point," he smiled. "I have some time to think about it, but it's an idea."

"I just—don't do this for me."

"Cami, I love baseball, you know that. But I love being with you more and I want to be a full-time husband and father."

"But there is not even a baby," I laughed.

He shrugged, "So? I had my superstar hay day. I wouldn't mind taking an entire season off, maybe, or more... I can coach little league or something. Would that be too boring for you?"

I shook my head, "I think you need to really think about this."

"I know," he nodded, and pulled me closer for another kiss.

I'm not going to lie and pretend I wouldn't love the idea of Drew always being in town. However, I still have my career and I don't want him to resent me for it. I know I get frustrated with my job sometimes, but it's as much a part of who I am as he and Ben are.

Besides, as a die-hard Yankees fan, I would be pissed if the co-captain decided to retire at thirty-two! My guess was Drew was scared he wouldn't be able to play the same after the injury, and wanted to take himself out of the game before someone else could.

Chapter Three

The next night, Drew and I sat on the couch watching ESPN where they kept showing the replay of the final game in the championship. Of course, the Yankees did sweep the Orioles, but instead of celebrating with his team, Drew had spent the night in the hospital.

Today, he had to deal with press interviews and the coaches planning a course of action with him being out of the most important games of the season. Drew felt like crap, and I knew it. Hell, I felt like crap for him, and for not being by his side through it all.

ESPN replayed Drew colliding with the runner, who he had tagged out, beating him to second base. Drew played hard that game, but he got hit even harder. In slow motion, the anguish on his face after he hit the ground with the runner landing onto his shoulder was enough to make you feel pain as well.

Drew changed the channel and I looked over at him. I squeezed his thigh and was about to say something, but my phone rang. I had decided to work from home for the next week to help Drew out. I could tell how bad he was hurting, both physically and mentally, but he didn't want me to see. He would pretend he wasn't in pain, and he didn't want to talk about baseball, but he kept watching game recaps and interviews with his teammates.

After I got off the one call, I had to dial in for a conference call. While I announced myself on the call, I saw Drew struggling to get comfortable on the couch. His shoulder was in a sling, along with an ice pack strapped into place. I checked the time and figured giving him painkillers fifteen minutes earlier than scheduled couldn't hurt.

I headed into the kitchen, grabbed a glass of water and two pills all the while listening to the conference call with Sound Wave. I walked over to Drew and held my hands out to him while cradling the phone between my ear and shoulder. Drew looked over to me, his brown eyes arguing with me that he was fine.

I practically shoved the pills and water at him. Sighing, he gave in, swallowing the pills quickly, and as if to prove he was okay, he stood up, pushing off the couch with his good arm, and disappearing into the kitchen. I heard the water running and curiously, I once again headed into the kitchen. Drew was one-handedly washing the glass he drank from. I tilted my head to the side, reached over and turned off the water before pointing toward the living room. He looked at me like a child in trouble and kissed my cheek before walking out.

I finished up the conference call a few minutes later, thankful it wasn't a long, drawn out one, and walked into the living room.

"Why are you being so stubborn?" I asked.

Drew laughed from his spot on the couch.

"Why are you?"

"I am trying to take care of you."

"Well, don't," Drew shrugged as best he could. "You have a career and a son to worry about, I'm fine."

I sat down next to him, tucking my legs underneath me.

"You are more important to me than my career. Don't you know that?" I asked.

He smiled and looked down. I turned his face toward me, horrified that he might not know that.

"Don't you?"

"Cami, I'm not offended. There was a time baseball was the most important thing in my life," he said, sadly.

"What changed?" I asked, but actually I was still baffled and offended how he could think my job was more important to me.

I desperately wanted Drew to say it was me who changed the value of the game. It was just like him to say something cheesy and make me swoon. The swooning never came though.

"I grew up," he simply said.

I stared at him, not happy with his answer for a couple of reasons.

"You grew up?" I laughed. "Drew... why are you being like this?"

"Like what?"

"Are you scared you won't be able to play again?"

Drew sighed, "I'm just accepting the fact that I won't play baseball forever. I gave up a lot of things for this sport, and maybe it's time to give up on it now."

"I never knew you to be a quitter," I said with a heavy sigh.

"I'm not quitting."

"It sure sounds like it."

"Give me a break, Cami. I'm not the only one to take myself out of a game."

"What does that mean?"

"Nothing," he closed his eyes.

"Drew, what did you mean?"

"I just think you're giving up on the idea of a baby without trying."

I shook my head and smacked my thigh, completely frustrated.

"Oh, really? How am I not trying? It's not like I'm on the pill…"

"It's your attitude about it," Drew said, staring at me.

"I can't talk to you right now," I said, standing up and hurrying to my bedroom.

I didn't get how we went from talking about his injury and baseball to my career and a baby! It was extremely rare I was upset with Drew, and that fact mixed with the sensitive topic of having a baby, made it all feel worse. I haven't cried in a while, but I sure was sobbing at that moment curled up in my bed. It was so easy for Drew to accuse me of having a bad attitude about a baby. He doesn't know what it feels like to have tried to conceive for years or to have a miscarriage. I have been through it all before and I was incredibly grateful to have Ben. He was such a little miracle and I was content with being just his mommy.

The doorbell rang and I knew it was Danny dropping off Ben. Drew could handle Danny's cold shoulder by himself, but I knew Ben would come looking for me. I slid off the bed and wiped my face before heading down the hallway.

"Sorry about your shoulder, bro," Danny said with Ben in his arms.

I couldn't believe Danny actually felt sympathy for Drew. If I wasn't upset with Drew, I'd be happy for him.

"Thanks, it'll be fine," Drew brushed it off.

"I want to show Mama my new suitcase!" Ben said, struggling to get down from his father's arms.

Tortured would be going on an eight week tour next month. Danny and I agreed it would be good for Ben to come along. I figured I'd make trips back and forth to New

York to see Drew, and he could visit too. Drew seemed cool with the idea since baseball season would be over, and he'd be with Jordan and me. I knew the tension between him and Danny would be there, but at least they're civil.

Ben came running toward me, with a rolling suitcase covered in super heroes.

"Mama, look what Daddy got me for the tour!"

"Wow!" I forced the biggest smile I was capable of. "That's so cool!"

I pulled my son into a hug and I didn't want to let him go. Tears were threatening to fall and I just wanted to bury my head into my little boy's shoulder, hoping he never grew up, and hurt girls' feelings with things he knew nothing about.

Danny walked closer, "I'll pick him up on Friday?"

I glanced up at him and nodded. Drew and Danny were both staring at me, knowing I was crying. I wasn't fooling anyone, not even Ben as he touched my cheeks.

"Why you crying, Mama?"

"I'm just happy to see you," I kissed his forehead. "Go bring your suitcase into your room."

Danny stepped even closer to me while Drew remained by the open door to our apartment.

"Are you okay?"

"I'm fine," I nodded.

Danny pulled me into a hug, "Call me if you need to talk."

I felt suffocated in his arms, but at the same time, I just wanted to bury my head in my ex-husband's chest, knowing he at least understood some of the hurt and struggle we had gone through trying to have a child.

"Thanks," I choked out before pulling away from him and looking at my feet.

Danny walked to the door and I glanced up to see him and Drew share a cold glare. Once the door closed, Drew ran a hand through his hair and I mumbled that I was starting dinner before going into the kitchen. The sounds of Ben pretending he was Batman could be heard from down the hall as I grabbed items from the refrigerator.

Drew walked into the kitchen and leaned against the island where I was placing carrots to be chopped.

"Can I help?"

"With one arm? No," I shook my head.

He walked around to me and wrapped his good arm around my back, pulling me against him.

"It kills me to not be able to wrap both arms around you," he kissed behind my ear before looking into my eyes. "I'm sorry."

My lip trembled, "About what? Accusing me of not wanting a child with you or my job being more important to me?"

"Cami, I wasn't saying the job thing offended me," he offered.

"It offended *me*, Drew," I pushed away from him. "I love you more than..." I sniffled and wiped my tears. "Do you want me to quit?"

"No, I don't want you to quit," he sucked his teeth. "I want you happy."

"Then why are you acting so weird?"

"I've just been thinking a lot," he said, running a hand over the surface of the island. "I got an invitation to my college reunion."

"Okay..." I waited for him to continue.

"I always wanted a family, but I chose baseball over a girl."

"This is about Katie?"

Katie Lawson was Drew's first and only love before me. He proposed to her and she said no because she couldn't handle his career.

"No, this is about us," he said, staring at me. "We're engaged and we'll be a family. I think it's time I settled down."

I rolled my eyes, "Drew, I'm not Katie. I love that you have a career you're passionate about. And I would love nothing more than to give you a baby."

He smiled at me and leaned over to kiss me.

"So you don't want me to quit baseball?"

"No!" I smacked his face, playfully.

He slapped my ass before pulling me against him.

"And you love me more than your career?"

"Duh," I laughed. "But if you care about someone, you would never ask them to make a choice between two things they love," I said, as a warning that I would not stand for him wanting me to choose between him and my job nor would I ever give him an ultimatum.

"You're amazing," he said, kissing my neck.

"You knew this already," I teased.

He looked into my eyes, "Between our engagement and the reunion coming up, I guess I just got spooked—like you would leave me or something."

"Drew, nothing could make me want to give you up," I said, laying a hand on his cheek. "You're the love of my life, and marriage or not, baby or not, whether you're retired or decide to play until you're sixty, we are a family no matter what."

He kissed me pressing me against the island, and I wanted to have him right then and there, but I could still hear Ben playing in his bedroom. Just as I was reminded of my son, I heard him charging down the hallway. I lightly pushed Drew back and pecked his lips just in time for Ben to enter the kitchen.

"Mama, can we watch a movie tonight?"

"Sure," I told him.

"Yes!" He cheered. "Drew, can you still play videogames with me?"

"Ben, no," I shook my head, but Drew obliged.

"Of course, I bet I can still beat you even with a bad shoulder."

"Nu-uh," Ben stuck his tongue out at him and took off toward his bedroom.

Drew looked back at me and winked before glancing down at the items I took out from the refrigerator.

"What are you making for dinner anyway?"

I laughed at the mismatched menagerie of food I took out while I was upset. Carrots, yogurt, and some leftover minestrone I had made over the weekend.

"Let's order out," I offered.

"Deal," Drew said before going to walk away.

"Wait, so when is your college reunion?"

"Drew!" Ben yelled.

"Hold on, buddy!" Drew called back before looking at me. "The weekend before Thanksgiving."

I would be on the tour by then, but figured I might be able to go.

"I'll be there," I smiled.

"It's no big deal," he shrugged. "I'm not even sure if I'm going to go."

Drew walked out of the kitchen and I began putting the items back in the refrigerator. My cell phone rang and it was Danny.

"Hey, did you forget something?" I asked when I picked up the call.

"I just wanted to make sure you were okay," Danny said.

I couldn't help but smile. As much as I wanted to throw Danny out the window, I appreciated how much he worried about me.

"I'm fine, thank you."

"Are you sure? You know I hate seeing you cry."

"I know. It was just a stupid fight Drew and I had."

"You need me to kick his ass?"

"You promised me you would never try anything like that again," I laughed.

"I would break that promise if it was to protect you," Danny said.

"Thank you," I said appreciatively. "I'll talk to you soon, D."

I hung up the phone and turned around to see Drew standing there. He looked at me as if I was doing something wrong.

"Danny was just making sure I was okay."

"Of course," Drew nodded, with what sounded like irritation in his voice. "I was just going to suggest Chinese for dinner."

"Sounds good," I smiled and he walked out of the room.

I sighed, not sure why Drew was in such a funk. I think the injury is upsetting him more than he is letting on.

Chapter Four

The Yankees had lost the World Series to the Phillies. Drew blamed himself and was making it difficult for me to be there for him. He didn't want me waiting on him while he was injured, and he didn't want to talk about his baseball future.

It was frustrating and I hated that he was being distant. We barely spoke about the wedding, and Drew and I kept busy spending time with the team, offering moral support.

Drew came out for the first week of the tour, but I was so busy that week along with Tortured, that he basically served as a babysitter for Ben and Jordan's dog. I can tell he felt neglected. Plus, Danny's cold shoulder seemed stronger than usual—or maybe Drew was giving him one now. He just wasn't himself and I didn't know how to handle it. He's usually the lighthearted one, and I didn't know how to offer that same attitude to him when it felt like he was pushing me away and brushing everything off.

He was supposed to stay with the tour an extra week, but he left to take part in a charity event. Maybe that would be good for him. Drew liked to help people, and I know he felt helpless injured and not being able to help his team out when it really counted. Of course, he never said that. He kept talking about baseball like he would never play again.

...

Tilly had her head down on my lap as I sat on the stage, catching up on emails. We were in Cincinnati and Tortured was at lunch while I stayed at the venue to do some work and make sure everything was in place for their show. Aside from Drew's depression or whatever it was, it felt great to be on the road again, and taking my son along for the ride. Ben loved having Danny and me in one place for a longer period of time.

I did miss Drew, though, even the mopey version of him. I would get to see him in a couple of days. Though he insisted his college reunion wasn't a big deal, I knew he was looking forward to it. I wanted to be there with him to meet his old buddies and to see him accept the "Hall of Fame" award the committee was granting him. And yes, I was curious to see Katie. In the four years they dated, I only met her a few times, but not remembering forming an opinion of her.

Danny walked over with a Styrofoam container of leftovers and sat down next to me. He scratched Tilly's head and tried to read over my shoulder, something he always did for as long as I could remember just to aggravate me. Without looking at him, I shoved him away with my shoulder and finished sending my email.

"Want some Skyline Chili?" he asked, holding out the leftover container.

I scrunched my face, "How can you eat that? That's not how Italians eat spaghetti."

He laughed and shrugged, "I like it. It's not your sauce, but it serves its own purpose."

I shook my head and Tilly groaned as if she agreed with me.

"Why does this dog love you so much?" Danny laughed as he rubbed Tilly's belly. She didn't remove her head from my lap, even as she turned over to give him access.

I rolled my eyes, "Beats the hell out of me. I have done nothing to provoke this."

Danny smirked, "Admit it, you secretly love how attached she is to you."

"Yeah, right!" I scoffed and looked down at the dog, who looked up at me and I laughed. "Why do you love me, Tilly?"

"Because she knows the truth about you," Danny smirked.

"What truth?"

"That underneath that tough, cold, sexy exterior, you're nothing but a big old mush."

I looked over at Danny and he stared into my eyes the way he does when he wants to get laid. Lately, he's been looking at me that way more often, and I am not sure how to stop it.

"Danny," I cleared my throat and pushed my hair behind my ears.

"Cami," he mimicked my tone and pushed my shoulder. "It was a joke. We all know you're not a mush," he said, brushing it off.

"Are you going to be on good behavior while I'm gone?" I asked.

"What are you talking about?"

"I'm talking about you and your extra-curricular tour activities while our son is with you on the road."

Danny stopped petting Tilly and leaned back onto his elbows.

"Have I done anything—or anyone—so far this tour?"

"Not that I know of, but it's only a few weeks in and you've been too busy making me uncomfortable with your comments," I smirked.

He laughed, and even blushed.

"Fair enough."

He looked over at me with those blue eyes of his and I will admit, my ex-husband is very good-looking. With the allure of his bad boy ways, it's no wonder I stayed with him so long. However, I know better now and I know I love Drew.

"Is this a game to you?"

"What are you talking about?" Danny played dumb.

"The looks, the comments—I'm engaged, remember?"

"I can't joke with you now that you're engaged?" he asked, using his fingers for quotation marks as he said the word "engaged" as if my commitment to Drew was fictional.

"You've gotten worse, and you know it," I sighed and he looked out into the seats.

Haley and Jordan walked into the venue hand in hand. Danny looked at them with envy.

"It's okay to admit you're lonely," I said delicately.

"I miss *you*, okay Cam?" Danny asked, looking back at me. "I miss *us* and it hurts to know you don't."

"D, you know we just didn't work. I love you, but..."

"I'm not golden boy, Drew. I get it," he cut me off bitterly.

"Oh, so I'm the bad guy now? Because I moved on? I fell in love with someone who is loyal, makes me high, and is actually *in* love with me, and you want to make me feel like crap for that?" I asked, about to get up.

Danny grabbed my hand to keep me from standing up. "I *am* in love with you, Cami. I never stopped being in love with you, but I always knew..." he swallowed. "I always knew you didn't feel the same way back."

I looked into those eyes; those same eyes that were there for me when I was hurting over Jordan, and I believed him—Danny was in love with me, in his own way I suppose, and from what he is saying, still is. He was right—I never felt that strongly about him.

Overwhelming guilt rushed through me, and I needed to get away from him. I yanked my hand away, and stood up, causing Tilly to look up perplexed. Without another word, I hurried down the stairs of the stage. I brushed past Haley and Jordan and headed for the tour buses.

Sebastian was playing catch with Ben in the parking lot, and I was thankful they didn't see me as I got onto my tour bus. I rushed to the back of the bus and plopped down onto the bed. My heart was racing and I wished Drew were there to hold me. I wanted to call him, but it was kind of hard to tell him my ex-husband told me he still loved me and that I felt terrible about it. Drew wouldn't feel sympathy; he would want to tell Danny to back away from me.

I forced myself not to call Drew. Instead, I gave myself ten minutes to cool down before getting off the bus and joining Sebastian and Ben.

"Hi Mama!" Ben yelled.

"Hi baby," I said and Sebastian looked at me.

"What has Drew been teaching him? He's throwing knuckle balls at me!"

I laughed, "Drew thinks he'll make a great pitcher."

"Mama, I miss Drew," Ben said.

"Me too, Ben."

"You get to see him this weekend at least," Sebastian said. "I won't get to see Tasha until next weekend," he sighed.

"Yeah, it's hard. Listen, is Danny okay?" I asked, realizing I bypassed his own yearning for his wife with other concerns.

He shrugged, "He's Danny. Is he ever okay?"

We both laughed.

"I mean—does he seem depressed to you?"

"Let's see, for the first time in his life, he's completely sober and single, so yes," Sebastian shrugged.

"I'm worried about him, Seb," I admitted.

"Cam, you know D. He'll be on the mend in no time."

"I just..." I paused.

"What?"

"Never mind. Just look out for him for me?"

Sebastian nodded, "Of course."

I pulled out my phone and scooped Ben up.

"Time for your interview," I told Sebastian and motioned with my head for him to follow me.

I met with the journalist at the door to the venue. He was some fresh-faced hipster straight out of college that *Bash Magazine* must have given a shot. He was one of those nerdy types that wanted to discuss the instrumentation of each song Tortured ever recorded. I kept checking the time, ready to cut the kid off after a half an hour. In the meantime, I kept Ben entertained in the hallway, which as much as I hate to admit it, was much easier with Tilly around. We played catch while the band gave probably the most boring interview of their careers with the nerdy, green journalist.

After the interview, I thanked the journalist, but he wanted to linger and talk about the first time he saw Tortured live and how much their music changed his life. Of course, Jordan indulged the kid and I even had to open up my mind somewhat. This was a huge moment for the kid—Michael—I think was his name.

"Thank you so much, Cami," he said to me. "I would love to sit down with you sometime for an interview."

"Me?" I laughed. "Why me?"

"Is that a serious question?" Michael asked. "You're like the biggest music manager in the industry."

"My ex-wife can be modest sometimes," Danny shot at me. "Sometimes oblivious."

"You're running late for sound check," I responded, glaring at him. "Michael, send me over any questions you may have for me," I told him, handing him my card.

As I did work on my phone while Tortured had sound check, Haley played a game with Ben while Tilly lay at my feet. I had a bad feeling in the pit of my stomach, and I wasn't sure why. Was it Danny's feelings for me that caused it? Or maybe it was Drew's reunion? I didn't feel any more comfortable about my fiancé seeing his first love again than I did with my ex-husband's somewhat unrequited feelings for me; that is if what Danny said was the truth.

Tilly put her snout in my lap as if she understood my feelings. I patted her head and she rubbed her head against my thigh, letting me know she enjoyed the contact. I suddenly felt bad for the dog who wanted so badly for me to love her back, and maybe, Danny was right, maybe in some way I do love Tilly, just like in some way I will always love him. But what killed me was knowing that in some way, Drew would always love Katie.

It wasn't like my love for Danny—we grew up together, we are raising a son together, we're family. No, Drew's love for Katie was everything for him—it was dreams of happily ever after and having a home and family he never had. She was it for him—all of his love and dreams were poured into Katie Lawson, and I would be stupid to think that could just end, or that it wouldn't rekindle once he saw her again. Maybe Drew's mood wasn't all about baseball, his injury and busy schedules. Maybe it was about him regretting what happened between him and Katie.

Chapter Five

I landed in LaGuardia Airport a little past seven a.m. Drew offered to pick me up, but I still wasn't keen on him driving with a bad shoulder, even though he wasn't wearing the sling any longer. He didn't complain much about pain and has adjusted to the injury. Still, I rather he have all fully working limbs while operating a vehicle in New York City traffic.

I walked into the apartment, expecting to find it a disaster. Other than a pair of dirty socks in the living room and a sink full of dishes, the place was spotless. I heard the shower running and a smile spread across my face, knowing how to kick start my time with Drew.

I dropped my bags in the hallway and fumbled with the buttons on my jacket, tossing it to the floor. I pulled off my boots and scarf before removing my t-shirt and skinny jeans, throwing it all in a pile next to my luggage. I yanked my socks off before sliding my panties down and finally removing my bra. I hate winter in New York—way too many items of clothing to remove.

I skipped off to the bathroom and opened the door. The steam made me choke and I heard Drew startle by slipping and dropping what sounded like the soap.

"Cami?" he called out.

"Who else?" I asked, stepping closer, admiring what I could see of his butt through the foggy shower doors.

"You got home quickly," he said with a smile, as I stepped into the shower.

I wrapped my arms around him and he pulled me into a kiss.

"I've missed you," I said, hugging him tight against my body.

I heard a strangled noise come from him and I pulled back.

"Did I hurt your shoulder?"

"Just a little," he said, kissing me again. "I missed you too." He pressed his forehead against mine.

I ran my hands down his back and squeezed his butt. He began kissing my neck before turning me around, and pulling me back against him.

"Can you feel how much I missed you?" he said seductively as he pressed himself against my butt.

I smiled, feeling all of the anxiety about the reunion, Katie, Drew's baseball funk, and Danny melt away as Drew's fingers caressed my breasts and kissed me. His fingers ran down my stomach before entering me, slowly and softly, causing me to moan. I reached for his erection and slid my hand up and down it a few times.

"I want you right now," I said, squeezing him, and leaning forward against the wall of the shower.

I missed the feeling of his fingers as he withdrew them, but not for long. Drew thrust himself inside of me much quicker and harder than he had with his fingers. I let out a loud squeak and he pulled himself out before pushing back in slowly, making me feel every inch of him.

Drew was great at providing a contrast of soft and slow, and fast and hard. It drove me crazy in the best way.

"I love you," I breathed. "So much."

Drew laughed in my ear and bit it softly.

"Don't throw around meaningless words during sex."

I sucked my teeth and pushed my butt back against him, causing him to groan as I squeezed him inside of me.

"Meaningless?"

He pulled my face to his and kissed me.

"I love you too."

I stared at him and as much as I wanted to continue what we were doing, I wondered if Drew's joke was something more. There was something in his tone of voice; something was off. Did he not think I truly loved him? I stepped away from him, and he slipped out of me.

"Water is getting cold," I said, stepping out of the shower and grabbing Drew's towel.

"Hey!" Drew said, as I wrapped the towel around myself and left the bathroom. "Cami!" he yelled after me.

I heard him almost slip behind me as he followed me to the bedroom. I was tackled to the bed and he ripped the towel off me and tossed it to the side. He must have thought I was playing around and teasing him—which I did love to do. He began kissing my neck and pushing my legs apart. He entered me again and tears filled my eyes. I willed myself not to cry, not sure why I was even crying. It was too soon for my period and I was too young for menopause, but I felt like I was in a hormonal tidal wave that I couldn't control.

Drew kissed me and I tried to kiss him back as tears streamed down my face. When he pulled back, I tried to bury my head into his chest, but he lifted my chin up.

"Why are you crying?" he asked, slowing down his movements.

I shrugged my shoulders as my lips trembled.

"I'm sorry," I whispered and he got off of me.

I rolled onto my side and curled myself into a ball.

"Talk to me," he said.

I rolled back toward him and put my head on his chest.

"I don't know where to start."

My words sounded muffled against his skin.

"Is it us? Are you having second thoughts about getting married?"

"No," I sniffled. "It's about you and Danny."

I don't know why I said that. My conversation with Danny was definitely on my mind, but so was many things that had nothing to do with him, and everything to do with Drew acting weird.

"Me and Danny?" he questioned and I looked up at him. "Cami, what's done is done."

"I'm afraid of hurting you and of hurting him."

"What do you mean?"

"Forget it. It's stupid," I said, remembering the reason I didn't want to explain Danny's feelings in the first place. I didn't want Drew to hash it out with him.

"Cami, just tell me!" Drew said annoyed.

His entire body was tense and when I looked at him, he had an expression on his face I couldn't place.

"Look, it's nothing. I'm just super emotional and Danny is hurting. He still confides in me and…"

"And maybe he shouldn't?" Drew asked. "So Danny is the reason you can't make love to me?"

I almost laughed. Drew looked incredibly outraged and I couldn't blame him. I pulled myself up and draped a leg over him.

"No," I sighed. "I just feel like I'm losing you."

"Are you crazy?!"

I shrugged, "Probably."

"Why would you think you're losing me?"

"Well, it's like you don't think I love you or something. The comment in the shower and that whole thinking my job was more important to me..."

He sighed and rubbed the back of my thighs softly.

"Baby, I know you love me."

"Do you?" I asked, seriously.

"Yes."

I sighed and looked into his eyes.

"Did you know Danny was in love with me?"

Drew rolled his eyes, "He was your husband."

"But I was not in love with him and he claims he was—and still is—in love with me."

"Why does he have to stir up old shit?" Drew groaned.

"I just feel bad that all this time I was never in love with him, and I kind of thought it was a mutual thing, and now..."

"Now, that crazy insecure brain of yours is thinking I don't know how much you love me?"

"Well, yeah."

Drew sighed and laughed.

"You're the love of my life," I told him, looking into his very confused brown eyes.

He pulled me down into a kiss and rolled me over onto my back. He may not think he needed to hear that, but I could see his face come back to life with my words that I truly meant.

"Prove it to me," he smirked and I laughed.

"I see that's where your brain is right now."

"It's been a couple of weeks!" he complained.

I smiled at him and reached my hands into his hair, pulling his face to mine. I kissed him with everything I had as I wrapped my legs around his waist. I moaned into his ear as he entered me once more. He stared into my eyes and I wanted to melt into him. The large pools of brown always sucked me in. I felt safe and loved and turned on all at once.

After we made love, I curled myself into his side and his large hand covered half of my butt. I sighed, content, happy to be in Drew's arms.

"Feel better?"

"Uh huh, you?"

"Yes."

I looked up at him, "But?"

"Well, I don't know exactly what crap Danny has been feeding you, but I don't like it."

"Drew, you know Danny. He's a baby sometimes and gets down on himself and lonely when he doesn't have anyone. So he turns to me," I blew it off.

Drew rolled his eyes, "So, you don't think he's still in love with you?"

"Probably not," I shrugged.

"Maybe you should keep your distance," he said, softly.

I laughed, "Right. I'll just avoid him on tour and have you or Jordan drop Ben off to him."

Drew sighed, "I'm not saying avoid him, but do you have to talk to him so much? You don't have to listen to him ramble on about his feelings. Walk away."

"Oh, because that's mature," I scoffed. "You still want to be friends with him, remember? Now, you don't want him to be *my* friend?"

Drew gently pushed me off him and got out of the bed. He went to the dresser and slipped on his boxer briefs.

"I don't know what you want me to say, Cami," he turned around and threw his hands up. "You come in here, seduce me in the shower, and end up crying about how I don't think you really love me and how your ex-husband still loves you. What the fuck?"

I sat up and sighed.

"Just forget I said anything, okay?"

"Sure. It's forgotten," he said, but looking pissed off.

He continued getting dressed as I just lay in bed, wanting to cut my tongue out for saying anything—and during sex, no less! This just wasn't my style. I'm pretty much a guy when it comes to sex; one-track mind and all business. With Drew, there was always more intimacy though. He showed me what intimacy was.

"I'll see you later," Drew threw over his shoulder as he walked out of the bedroom.

"Where are you going?"

Drew walked back into the room.

"Some of my college buddies are getting some drinks. Maybe when I get back we can set a date for the wedding or do you have to check with Danny on that? I wouldn't want to hurt him, you know?"

"You're being an asshole," I sighed.

"Good," he said, and from his body language, it was clear how livid he was. "That makes two assholes in this relationship."

My mouth dropped and Drew stormed down the hallway.

"Yes, I called you an asshole, Cami!" he yelled before slamming the door behind him.

...

I lay in bed with so many thoughts racing through my mind. I knew exactly what I was doing. I was causing problems in my relationship that weren't even there. Or were they? Drew's right; I'm insecure. The weird part is I'm more secure of Drew's feelings for me than I am of my feelings for him. I hate to say that, but I spent a good portion of my life in a relationship with Danny, and I never loved him the way I should. Worse than that, I harbored feelings for Jordan all of that time. What kind of person does that make me? I'm so damn afraid to be Drew's wife because I know he will make the best husband in the world, and I don't know if I can consider myself a good wife. I seemed to have made Danny miserable, even if he does claim to still be in love with me.

What if in ten years I realized I never truly loved Drew and I hurt him? What if love is such a fleeting feeling that it will just fade? I can't imagine never loving Drew. I can't imagine never wanting him in every way possible, even if he did just call me an asshole!

Ugh. I'm absolutely crazy! Here I am, engaged to the sexiest, most amazing man and on the night before he is seeing his ex-girlfriend for the first time, I give him a bunch of crap. I really should have been talking to him about what was putting him in such a weird mood lately. Was it baseball?

Me? The baby he wants with me? Instead, I threw this whole Danny drama into the mix, and made it all about me. Ugh, I *am* an asshole!

I threw on a t-shirt and sweat pants before I picked up my phone. I called Haley, praying she would answer.

"Hey Cami, you miss the tour that much?" she answered with a laugh; being that it was only hours since I last saw her.

"Actually, I miss girl talk," I sighed.

"What's wrong?"

"I pissed Drew off."

"You've been home for like two seconds!" she laughed again.

"I know. I'm just... I don't know why I'm feeling so crazy lately. I'm crying a lot; I'm angry, empathetic..."

"Empathetic?" Haley asked, sounding alarmed.

I rolled my eyes, "I know, so out of character for me."

She laughed yet again, "Cami, I was teasing. No one thinks you're as bitchy as you think you are."

"Well, thanks I guess."

"So what happened with Drew?"

"It's his reunion—it has me worried about Katie, and then Danny had to go and tell me he's in love with me, and I'm freaking out."

"Oh Danny," she sucked her teeth. "Listen, we love the guy, but I wouldn't dwell too much on things he says when he's lonely. Besides, it's not your problem he can't move on. Don't ruin what you have with Drew over whatever Danny is feeling..." she said before pausing. "Wait, do you still feel something for Danny?"

"No, I mean—I love him like I love you, but—"

"You love me?" she squeaked. "I don't think you ever told me that!"

"Shut up, you know I love you," I laughed. "Anyway, I love Danny like family, but I never knew he was in love with me. I thought our love/hate thing was mutual all these years. Now, I'm worried Drew and me—what if one of us loves the other one more?"

Haley was quiet for a moment.

"Do you think Drew loves you more?"

"I don't know. I love him so much I am so scared to lose him, and I feel like I'm pushing him away and am not very good at showing him."

"Cam, you proposed to him. I think that says something huge to him. Now, if you two can set a date, and not let your jealousy get in the way—"

"What jealousy?"

"Um, yours over Katie—who hasn't been in the picture in like ten years, by the way," she said, thinking I was being ridiculous. "...And Drew definitely is jealous of Danny."

"He told you that?"

"Well, not in so many words, but I can see it anytime Danny is talking to you. You and Danny, as much as you two fight, share a strong bond that Drew feels left out of. I think that's partly why he wants a baby with you so much."

I thought about Haley's words and it made so much sense. As much as I am scared of losing Drew, he's afraid of losing me too. That's why we've both been acting weird, though I still think something is up with my hormones.

I sighed, "I never thought about that."

The doorbell rang, startling me.

"Hay, someone's at the door. I'll talk to you soon, okay?"

"Okay. Tilly misses you by the way."

I laughed, "Don't tell anyone, but I kind of miss her too."

"I knew it!" Haley yelled before I hung up on her.

I hurried to the door, hoping it was Drew. Maybe he had forgotten his key and came back to make love again instead of visiting with beer-bellied old frat brothers. I opened the door, surprised to see Aylin standing there on the verge of tears.

"What's wrong?" I immediately asked.

Her face crumbled and she buried her head into my shoulder. I squeezed her softly before closing the door behind her.

"I'm sorry for coming here, but I didn't want to call my parents and—my friends just won't get it," Aylin sobbed out.

When it came to emotions, she was all Haley. She wore her heart on her sleeve and you can see whatever she was feeling on her face, which I would imagine was more of a curse than a blessing. Jordan always knew what Haley was feeling, and I bet that was frustrating when you wanted to pretend like nothing was wrong—like I did most of my life.

"You never have to apologize for coming here, A," I said, leading her into the living room.

We sat down on the couch and Aylin sighed as she wiped her eyes.

"I feel like it's wrong—you're my parents' friend and Uncle Drew... is he here?"

"He went out, but listen, I may be your mom and dad's friend, but I'm still your aunt. We're family," I assured her. "You can talk to me—no judgment."

Although I said those words, I feared Aylin would drop a bomb on me that she wanted to keep secret from her parents. It would most certainly put me in an awkward position. At the same time, I was flattered Aylin trusted me and I would hate for her to feel alone in any situation.

"Thank you," she sniffled. "You know how Rad and I've been hanging out?"

"Yes," I said, staring into her teary green eyes, already imagining the million ways I could destroy Rad Trick's career.

"Well, we were just friends, but he kissed me a few times and I just didn't feel anything. I tried to explain that to him tonight after he was pushing me to go further and kept trying to kiss me."

"What did he do, Aylin?" I asked, my jaw tightening.

"He basically flipped out on me and told me I was a tease and how he has feelings for me. He said that I played with him and now I just feel bad. He won't return my calls or anything," she said, and I was relieved it wasn't something else that happened.

I patted her knee.

"Aylin, you can't change your feelings and at least you were honest with him."

"But Aunt Cam, I feel awful. I should have said something the first time he kissed me, but I thought it was just a fluke or if he did it again, maybe I'd feel differently. Rad's right, I led him on. I'm a terrible person."

I smiled at her, "Listen to me, you are a beautiful person with a big heart. You didn't want to hurt him, and I think Rad will get over it. Just give him some time, but it might not be a good idea to stay friends right now. That might lead to hope that something will change in the future."

"We can be friends eventually though, right? I mean—you and Dad stayed friends—"

"How did you know I dated your father?" I asked, shocked.

Aylin rolled her eyes, "Please, I know everything."

I eyed her suspiciously, "Who told you?"

"Mom told me."

I shook my head, "She told you how mean I was to her when we met, didn't she?"

"She said you were a little cold," Aylin shrugged, and laughed through her tears. "But she also said she respected how protective you and Uncle Danny were of Dad and the band."

"We're family—like I said."

I imagined at this moment, my mother was laughing in heaven. She always talked about family and how important it was to protect it. "Famiglia" was a part of our daily Italian dinner blessing. I don't remember it all, but it started with "Dio" and "Famiglia" and ended with "mangia".

"Listen, Aylin, it took me a very long time to accept that your father would never be mine," I admitted. "It's very hard to get over someone you still see all the time."

"What about Uncle Danny?"

I had to laugh now. Could this conversation have any better timing?

"Uncle Danny and I are dysfunctional, and now, we are linked together by Ben and I work with him."

"So, not trying to cause trouble, but do you still have feelings for him?"

I shook my head, "Not like that, no. Again, to be honest, I never loved him like I should have. Not like I love your Uncle Drew."

Aylin smiled softly and put her hand on my arm.

"You know exactly how I feel then."

"I do," I nodded. "I care so much about Danny and I don't know how to take his pain away."

Aylin pulled me into a hug and I felt bad that she came to me for comforting, but somehow she's consoling me. We pulled apart and both laughed as we wiped tears.

"You want to go out for some Frrrozen Hot Chocolate?" I asked her.

"Sure," Aylin shrugged.

...

I fixed myself up and we headed a few blocks down to Serendipity. Thankfully, it wasn't too crowded, like it usually is. I figured we'd be safe considering it was ten p.m. on a Thursday night. With that said, we still had to wait ten minutes for a table.

We were seated and both knew what we wanted. The regular Frrrozen Hot Chocolate for me, and the peanut butter one for Aylin. Danny and I used to take Aylin to Serendipity any time we babysat her, and she always ordered the same thing, insisting she could finish an entire giant frosty glass of the rich concoction by herself; in actuality, she could never finish it.

As she tried to get down the last half of her icy drink, I could tell nothing had changed. She may be nineteen, but Aylin Ashton was so much the little girl we all adored. I would have to remind her parents of that next time they worry too much.

Usually I shared my Frrrozen Hot Chocolate with someone, but I had no trouble finishing it all by myself that night. I was PMSing, after all, and probably stress eating—well, drinking.

"Thank you Aunt Cami," Aylin said as she stood in front of the subway entrance tucking her hands into her gloves.

I rubbed my arms, "I can't tell if it's really this cold or I'm still chilled from the Frrrozen Hot Chocolate."

Aylin laughed, "Me neither."

It was the middle of November and New York was already in winter mode, with snow forecasted for this weekend.

"Get home safe and don't beat yourself up," I hugged her.

"You either," she winked and I laughed.

I waited until Aylin disappeared down the stairs before heading back to my apartment building. I smiled to myself, thinking about Drew, and making up with him. I hated that I let my fears get the best of me.

I stopped into the corner drugstore and walked down the feminine care products aisle. I picked up a pregnancy test and sighed. I suddenly had an urge to take a test, even though I was afraid of negative results. True, I could just be PMSing, but what if my heightened emotions could mean something else?

Chapter Six

I fell asleep waiting up for Drew. When I woke up, he was not in bed. I walked into the master bathroom and looked at myself in the mirror. I chickened out of taking the pregnancy test. There was no way I could mentally handle a no last night, and this morning, I felt sick to my stomach—which almost makes me happy, if it's morning sickness, but really, I know it's from finishing the entire Frrrozen Hot Chocolate, and taking a few sips of Aylin's as well.

Maybe Drew would be in the mood for a workout today. I brushed my teeth and hair before seeing Drew passed out on the couch with the YES! Network on the television. I turned off the T.V. and Drew's eyes fluttered open.

"Hi."

He rubbed his eyes, "Hey."

"You were right," I sighed.

"About?"

"Me being an asshole."

He laughed, "Don't call my fiancée an asshole."

I smiled and sat down in his lap. He kissed my lips softly and I hugged him.

"I'm scared," I admitted, though the words were muffled into Drew's neck.

"Me too," he said, running his fingers through my hair.

We stayed like that for a few moments—just me, curled into his lap feeling content in comforting each other in our relationship fears.

"Did you have fun last night with your buddies?"

"Um, it was okay," he said.

I looked at him and he brushed my hair off my shoulders.

"I kept thinking about you and how much I just wanted to be with you."

I smiled and kissed him, like it had been years since the last time. He pushed me back onto the couch and got on top of me.

"I am so in love with you that I can't think straight," I breathed as I helped pull his shirt over his head.

He smiled, "I am so in love with you I actually feel physical pain when you're not with me."

I knew that feeling well. There were certain days that I just needed Drew next to me, and I could feel his absence with my whole body.

I pulled him down into another kiss and thought how sickeningly crazy in love we are. How could I doubt anything about us? We made love with all of this extra passion and need that it felt like nothing could come between us. We are united and nothing else could be right, but us right there in that moment together.

Afterward, we lay on the couch, half asleep. My stomach grumbled and Drew chuckled.

"What would you like for breakfast?"

"Anything you give me," I said sleepily.

He kissed my cheek and carefully got off the couch, trying not to disturb me. I caught a glimpse of his naked butt before he slipped his boxers on and headed into the kitchen. I slowly got up a few minutes later and threw on my clothes. As we ate breakfast—egg whites and smoked maple tempeh—a vegan product Haley turned Drew onto, which was decent enough, we chatted about the tour and baseball.

Drew said the physical therapist offered hope that he would be back in time for the start of spring training. For the first time since his injury, I heard the hope return to Drew's voice, as well as that drive he has for his career.

I told him about my bond with Tilly getting worse—he saw some of it while he was on the tour, but she didn't leave my side after he was gone. I didn't mention Danny and neither did he. It was as if we both wanted to avoid talking about him and his feelings; right now, that was probably best.

We got ready for the day and met up with Matt Porter and his wife Laura for lunch. Matt and I tried not to talk business, but it was a challenge. Our children were safer.

"We need to schedule plenty of play dates when you guys come to town for spring training," Laura said. "Maddie misses Ben."

Matt and Laura lived in Tampa with their daughter, but spent a fair amount of time in Los Angeles and New York. When

Yankees spring training starts, I usually go to Tampa with Drew and Ben for a month.

"I don't know how much time in Tampa I'll get next year," I warned. "We're working on a UK tour for Tortured. Danny really wants Ben to come—which means I'll hang around more than usual."

I looked at Laura and Matt when I spoke, but I saw their eyes drift to Drew. I looked at him as well, and wondered if he had made a displeased face, but he just had a fake smile on instead.

"But I will definitely be in town for some of spring training," I added.

"I'll be down for hanging out," Drew said.

"How's the shoulder doing?" Matt asked.

"It's good; almost as good as new."

Toward the end of lunch, Drew got up to use the restroom. Matt took that as an opportunity to pry.

"Everything okay?"

"Fine," I shrugged, taking a sip of water.

He squinted his blue eyes and leaned closer.

"Did you two have a fight?"

"Matt, leave her alone," Laura scolded him.

"If you must know, yes, we fought last night, but we're fine now," I smiled.

"You sure?" Matt continued. "Drew seemed tense about you being on the Tortured tour."

I shrugged, "It's fine. We're fine."

"So, did you set a date yet?" Laura asked.

"We were supposed to last night," I sighed. "Between fighting and making up... it just didn't happen," I laughed.

When Drew came back to the table, I felt like I was going to throw up. My stomach was in worried knots. The fear I had of losing Drew was eating me from the inside. I knew fear could be deadly in any situation. We just had to get through the reunion and the rest of the tour, and start planning the wedding—the jitters and hang-ups will disappear by then.

We parted ways from Matt and Laura and got inside a taxi. Silence filled the car until my phone went off. I looked at the phone and of course it was Danny. I didn't want to answer it, but since Ben was with him, I worried it had something to do with him.

"Hello?" I picked up.

"Hey," Danny said.

"What's up?"

"I wanted to apologize."

"For?"

I felt Drew's eyes on me. I'm sure he could make out Danny's voice through the phone.

"Laying all that stuff on you."

"Apology accepted. Can we talk later?"

"Oh sure. Ben wants to say hi quickly."

I glanced over at Drew and his jaw tightened.

"Hi Mama!"

"Hi baby boy," I smiled when I heard my son's voice.

It was the only comfort I had right now while my fiancé was shooting me dirty looks and my ex-husband felt guilty for his feelings.

"Mama, Daddy and Uncle Sebie took me to the zoo!"

"Wow, what kind of animals did you see?"

Ben went on to list all the animals he saw before he went on to speak about baseball.

"I've been practicing just like Drew told me to!"

I looked over at Drew and he smiled, hearing Ben practically screaming through the phone.

"Do you want to talk to him and tell him?" I asked.

"Yes, I wish you and Drew were here," Ben said.

"I know, baby, hold on."

I handed Drew the phone and could hear Ben rambling on about the past couple of weeks on the tour.

"All right, I promise to see you soon, buddy. Maybe I'll come out and visit you on the tour again."

Drew hung up the phone and handed it back to me. I put my head down on his shoulder and he wrapped an arm around me.

"How about New Year's Eve?" Drew asked.

"For what?" I looked up at him.

"Our wedding," he smirked.

I sat up and stared at him.

"Seriously? That's less than two months away!" I laughed.

He shrugged, "So what? We don't need a huge event. I just want to marry you already and I know we both have off for a few weeks around that time."

I thought about it for a moment before leaning in and kissing him.

"It's a date."

"Really?" he asked surprised.

"Yes," I smiled, feeling relief wash over me.

I had nothing to fear. No fear. That will be my daily affirmation. Nothing can hurt Drew and me... Another affirmation I need to make daily.

Chapter Seven

That night, I made sure I pulled out all of the stops to look sexy. I just hope my insecurity wasn't worn across my pushed up chest. I stared at myself in the mirror and knew that my looks were not the issue. My short, tight, red dress and my icy blue eyes could attract men—I knew that from experience. Even in my forties, it was obvious my exotic look let me get away with just about anything. However, I also knew from experience that no matter how good I looked, that didn't secure a man. Danny still strayed.

That was when I finally realized I needed to focus on my inner self. Drew helped me do that. He made me believe I was a good person.

As I looked in the mirror, though, wondering about all the history that would come back up when Drew saw Katie for the first time in ten years, could I really compete with her? I knew she was nothing like me inside and out.

I felt Drew's arms wrap around me from behind and I closed my eyes, silently praying I'd always feel those arms around me.

"You are smoking," he said, grazing my neck with his teeth.

I smiled and looked at him in the mirror, "Is it too much?"

"Well, I can tell I'll be smacking a lot of my old buddies for looking at you, but you're going home with me," he winked.

I turned around and looked into his brown eyes before kissing him.

"I just have to go to the bathroom and then we'll go."

I nodded and Drew went off to the bathroom. I grabbed my purse and walked toward the door. Drew came out a moment later.

"Cam, um, is there something you want to tell me?"

I looked at him funny.

"Um, not that I can think of?"

"There's a pregnancy test in the medicine cabinet."

I chuckled, "Oh, I bought that the other night."

"Any reason why?" he asked, his eyes hopeful and a smile playing on his lips.

I shrugged, "Wishful thinking."

"Why didn't you take the test?"

"I'm afraid of rejection," I sighed. "I don't like being told no," I pouted.

He stepped closer to me, "Do you think you could be pregnant?"

I sighed, "I don't know, Drew. I've been super emotional, and I can't tell if that's because of hormones or something else."

Drew nodded, "Come on, let's go."

I could tell he wanted to talk more about the topic, but tonight wasn't the night. He took my hand and we headed downstairs to catch a car to Midtown. Drew's alma mater is Stony Brook University on Long Island, but the banquet is being held at a hotel.

"You know, I've been thinking," Drew said as we sat in the black sedan.

I looked over at him, waiting for him to continue.

"Maybe we should start going to a therapist."

I blinked a few times, wondering if I heard him correctly. A therapist? Did Drew think I was crazy? Did he think our arguments were so severe we needed therapy?

"You're worried about us?" I swallowed.

"I just think before we get married it might be good for us to get rid of some of our demons."

"I don't have demons," I said, offended.

"Cami, everyone has demons. You and I both have hang-ups and baggage from past relationships—my parents included in that baggage."

"So this is to help you?" I wondered, knowing his parents neglected him. "Well, then sure."

Drew scoffed and rolled his eyes, "Right, yeah, I'm the only one who needs therapy."

I scowled at him, "Considering I'm the one who had to propose, I would say, yeah—you have some blocks."

Drew let out a heavy sigh and I could tell he was pissed. I tried to take his hand in mine, but he pulled away from me.

"I'm sorry," I said softly.

"Me too," he mumbled, still not looking at me.

"Look, we can talk more later. I didn't mean..."

Drew looked over at me and nodded.

"Maybe neither one of us is ready to get married."

I stared at him speechlessly, hating that he said it, but also hating myself for thinking he was probably right. The car pulled up to the hotel and a doorman opened his door. Drew stepped out and I tried to keep it together as I followed behind him. I quickly took his hand in mine and he allowed it as we walked inside the hotel.

There was a small group of paparazzi snapping our picture and calling out to Drew about whether or not he would play next season. We pretended they didn't exist. Most of the time, Drew at least would give them something, but this wasn't the place, and after the conversation he and I just had, it definitely wasn't the time.

So many people were coming up to Drew once we got inside. People I'm sure he didn't even know in college, but of course, they knew him. I played the part—smiling politely at whomever I was introduced to, but ultimately, keeping quiet.

Mentally, I checked out. I was back in the car, hating my responses to Drew, and still feeling conflicted at his suggestion of therapy. I certainly felt crazy sometimes, but I was highly offended to think my fiancé thought I needed a therapist. Then again, he said *we*, not me. Ugh, I'm so self-absorbed and stubborn.

I had completely zoned out as Drew talked to some old baseball teammates when I spotted a tall, red headed woman walking toward me. It was as if the crowd parted for her. She had vibrant green eyes, a waif like figure and looked more like a teenager than a woman in her thirties. Though I have only met Katie Lawson a handful of times years ago, I somehow was able to spot her out in a large crowd.

People stopped her as she kept her eyes on Drew—*my* Drew. She was eloquent and porcelain. She was probably my exact opposite in every way possible.

She passed me without a glance and tapped Drew—*my* Drew—on his back. A dainty little tap that he probably barely felt, but maybe he missed her long little fingers on his skin, as he turned around and his face lit up when he saw her.

I wanted to cry. I couldn't help it. I knew my reaction to this moment was crucial to the future of my relationship with Andrew Ashton. If I made a scene, he would never forgive me. If I made a scene, I would prove his crazy theory right, though he never called me crazy—I was the one who kept calling myself that. I felt insane with jealousy as I watched Drew hug this woman he once loved.

I was not very good at playing nice. I never was. Swallowing down my emotions, I took a step forward as Drew—*my* Drew—I reminded myself mentally once more—complimented Katie on how she looked, and she returned the compliment. She even ran her hand down his chest as she told him how great he looked. I truly wanted to smack her; if this were twenty years ago, I would have.

"This must be Katie," I practically shouted enthusiastically, with a smile too big to fit my face.

Katie looked at me oddly, like she was trying to remember if I was one of her classmates.

"Katie, this is Cami—my fiancée," Drew said.

I couldn't help but hear a twinge of anger in how he said the word fiancée, like he was thinking of changing that status to ex-girlfriend.

"Oh!" Katie shouted, somewhat like I did. "It's so nice to finally meet you."

"We actually met a few times before," I managed to say, reminding myself to play nice.

"Right, now I remember," Katie nodded, but I could tell she probably didn't recall me too much. "Drew's told me so much about you," she said, hugging me.

I wanted to rip away from her, but I refrained and then her words hit. Drew has talked to her? When? I didn't know they kept in touch.

"He did, huh?" I asked, smirking over at Drew.

He rolled his eyes as if to tell me I had nothing to worry about.

"Katie came out with us last night."

"Oh, did she?" I asked, gritting my teeth.

"She did," he nodded.

Katie must have noticed our tension.

"I'm going to get a drink," she said, looking between Drew and me. "Would anyone like one?"

"I would love one," Drew grinned.

"Still drinking Heineken or have your tastes refined since making the big leagues?" Katie asked, and I wanted to punch her and her stupid way of flirting.

"I never change," he winked.

Ugh! Now Drew was flirting back and right in front of my face! I wanted to punch him.

"Cami?" Katie asked.

"No, thanks," I told her, though I really wanted to have a drink on hand just in case I wanted to throw it in someone's face.

I knew drinking would just lead me to feeling even worse than I already do. I shoved Drew as soon as Katie walked away.

"You said you went out with the guys last night! I can't believe you lied to me!"

"Shh," Drew hushed me, and tried to wrap his arms around me.

I pushed him back and went to walk away, but he grabbed my arm.

"Cami, please be mature about this."

I turned to him and took a deep breath.

"Why did you lie to me?"

Drew looked anywhere, but in my eyes and I knew that wasn't a good sign.

When he finally looked at my face, he had tears in his eyes and I wanted to throw up.

"I had to see her without anyone else around," he said, swallowing. "We've been emailing the past few weeks."

I couldn't believe this was happening. I know I am outrageously jealous and fearful, but to have those feelings justified did not make me feel good at all.

"Why Drew?" I asked, hearing the tremble in my voice.

"To see if anything was still there."

I nodded, "Right, of course. And?"

"I love you very much, Cami," he said and I couldn't choke back the cry that was in my throat.

Just then, Katie walked over with two drinks in her hand. The hateful part of me wanted to take both of those drinks and dump one on her and one on Drew, but instead, I turned and fought my way through the crowd, which was not easy to do. I kicked my shoes off and grabbed them in my hand, thankful I didn't check my jacket yet, as I hurried out of the hotel.

I felt incredibly humiliated. I didn't want to face all of these unfamiliar faces, and

I certainly didn't want to look at Katie's or Drew's, knowing I was the third wheel.

It was like everything I feared came true, after I told myself I was just paranoid, after Drew acted like I was the one causing problems. Drew is in love with Katie Lawson, and maybe he never stopped loving her, but now that he's reunited with her—I am shit out of luck. As I hopped into a taxi, I locked the door and Drew caught up. He pounded on my window and I could hear him yell my name.

I could barely see Drew with all of the blinding flashes going off behind him as the photographers enjoyed the very public scene going on between the Yankees co-captain and his music mogul fiancée.

"Go!" I barked at the driver.

I wanted to curl up on the seat and disappear. How could this happen again? I imagined the headlines for the next day. The paparazzi had plenty of photos of Drew chasing me to the taxi. If being cheated on by two different men weren't bad enough, the public humiliation would do me in. My tough image and pride was everything in my career.

When I got back to the penthouse, I didn't know what to do. I just knew I couldn't wait there for Drew to come back. He had called my phone three times before I turned it off. I decided I needed to be with family. I grabbed my suitcase that was never unpacked in the first place and called for a car to take me to the airport.

I caught the red eye to Nashville and called Danny as soon as I landed. I didn't know who else to call; I needed family and Tortured was my only family. I didn't want to go to Jordan and Haley—not about Drew, not now anyway. While I was close to Sebastian and Darren, I just needed something more—someone to be angry with me and not feel sorry for me.

"Cami?" Danny answered, sleepily.

"Sorry to wake you. I'm on my way to your hotel."

"What?" he asked surprised. "I thought you were coming back next week."

"Long story. I just—I need a friend."

"Of course. I'll be waiting for you."

I arrived at the Loews Vanderbilt Hotel and took the elevator up to Danny's room. When he opened the door, I hurried inside and dropped my suitcase.

"How's Ben?"

"He's good. Sound asleep in the bed. Are you okay?" Danny asked.

I turned around and allowed my purse to fall from my shoulder.

"No," I said looking at him.

He wore a white tank top, and a silver chain across his chest with flannel pajama pants. He still looked the same as he did when we were kids, but with a slightly more distinguished face and a Clooney-esque dusting of silver mixed into his dark hair.

I remembered why I was drawn to him when we first started dating as he wrapped his long arms around me. I fit into him like a child. At eighteen, after my heart hurt over Jordan, and never having a father in my life, this hug felt like it could solve all my problems. I felt protected.

The feeling was still there, even though I was no longer a teenager, I was still seeking comfort and protection.

"Do you want to talk about it?" Danny asked, still hugging me.

"No," I sniffled as I cried into his chest and squeezed him tighter.

I don't know how long we remained in each other's arms, but we didn't pull apart until I heard Ben call to me.

"Mama!" He yelled running to me and hugging my legs.

I quickly wiped my tears as I pulled away from Danny, seeing I soaked his tank top. I scooped Ben up and he squeezed me.

"Come on, let's get some sleep," I said to Ben and looking at Danny, reaching my hand out to him, and pulling him toward the bed with us.

I lay Ben down in the middle of the bed. I took off my jacket and kicked off my shoes. Danny glanced over my revealing dress as I lay down next to Ben.

"Mama, you look pretty."

I smiled and kissed his forehead.

"Thank you, baby boy."

Ben snuggled close to me and I looked at Danny.

"Sleep with us," I said.

"Are you sure?"

I nodded and Danny got into the bed, somewhat carefully. I felt his arm wrap around Ben and me. I stared into his eyes, not knowing whether to feel guilt or comfort at the moment we were sharing as a family.

The sense of security outrode the guilt though—and so did the thoughts of what Drew and Katie might be doing or already have done.

Chapter Eight

I sat at IHOP the next morning while Danny stared at me as I barely ate. Ben played with his pancakes and Danny scolded him—something I normally did, but was too out of it to care about at the moment.

"Are you going to talk to me?"

I looked at Danny and saw the concern on his face.

"Drew and I had a fight," I shrugged.

Danny nodded and sighed. He leaned back in the booth like he was annoyed and I groaned.

"What?"

"I don't appreciate you running to me because you and your fiancé had a spat."

"I didn't run to you," I sucked my teeth.

"You didn't?" he laughed. "You caught a flight in the middle of the night and wound up in my bed."

I sighed, "I wanted to be around my family. In case you didn't know, I consider you family," I said, looking into his eyes.

Danny nodded, "I know, but... I just told you I still love you. Don't you think this messes with me?"

Now I leaned back in the booth, feeling worse than before.

"I'm sorry."

"Don't be. I'm glad you still come to me, but it just sucks because in the end I know how you feel about me."

"Danny," I said, putting my hand on top of his and squeezing. "I do love you. I can't imagine you not being in my life, and you have given me the greatest gift anyone could give me."

We both looked over at Ben who had whipped cream all over his mouth. We laughed and Danny wiped our son's face before looking back over at me.

"I love you, too, Cam," he said, squeezing my hand back. "I'm sorry I wasn't a better husband and I'm really sorry Drew hurt you."

I shrugged, "I just didn't expect it from him."

Danny rolled his eyes, "But you expected it from me, of course."

I laughed, "Well..."

He squeezed my hand tighter and I winced, pulling my hand away.

"I just—Drew was—"

"Perfect?" Danny asked. "No one is perfect, Cami. Everyone makes mistakes and I don't know what he did, but I have no doubt that Drew loves you."

I looked at my ex-husband and hoped I didn't hurt him more with these words.

"Love isn't enough. I know Drew loves me. I want loyalty. I want to know I am the only one."

Danny nodded, "He cheated on you?"

"I'm not sure."

"You're not even sure and you came running here?"

"He lied to me, Danny."

Danny nodded and just then his phone rang.

"Hey J, what's up?" He answered. "Yeah, Cami flew in last night. She's right here. Alright, we'll be there soon."

I looked at him expectantly.

"Drew called Jordan looking for you."

I nodded, not surprised.

"Are you going to face your fiancé or what?"

"Not yet. I'll see what his brother has to say first."

...

A little while later, we were back at the hotel. I walked over to Jordan and Haley's room and knocked. Jordan opened the door and looked at me as if I was the one in trouble.

"Don't look at me like I'm wrong," I said walking into his room.

Tilly came running over and I welcomed the happiness radiating off the dog that was excited to see me. I gave her a few pets before looking over at Jordan.

"Where's Haley? I need a female on my side."

"She flew out early this morning," Jordan said. "She had a last minute photography gig in L.A."

"Great," I said sarcastically. "Go ahead and tell me I'm dumb and jump to conclusions."

He closed the door and turned to me.

"Look, you have every right to be upset. Drew lied to you about seeing Katie, but that doesn't mean anything happened between them. Give him some credit. He's not Danny," Jordan said.

I sighed, "I know he's not Danny, but I also saw the look on his face. Something is going on that he feels awfully guilty about."

Jordan didn't respond to that, which led me to believe he agreed.

"Running away is not the answer. You made a very public scene. Have you seen the tabloids?"

"I don't fucking care about the tabloids, Jordan!" I yelled. "My heart is broken. And this isn't like what it felt like with Danny at all—this is worse. I love Drew with everything inside of me and I don't know how to recover from that," I said, breaking down into a sob.

Jordan pulled me into a hug.

"Recover from what? You don't even know what Drew is feeling because you're so afraid to hear what he has to say."

I pulled away from Jordan and wiped my face with my sleeve before letting out a few deep breaths. I felt woozy.

"I feel sick," I said, hurrying to the bathroom and leaning over the toilet.

Nothing came out and that made me feel worse. Jordan walked into the bathroom.

"I'm worried about you."

"I'm fine—just a little wishful thinking morning sickness," I said sarcastically.

"When did you last get tested?" Jordan wondered.

I shrugged, "I don't know."

"Maybe it's time to take a test," he suggested.

"No, I can't take any more bad news," I refused.

"Cami," Jordan groaned. "Something is up with you!"

"Your brother is in love with another woman! That is what's up with me!" I yelled.

"Look, Drew told me you've been acting weird..."

"Right, it's all me—he's been perfectly normal," I said.

"I know you're scared of losing Drew, but you running away from him is not going to help."

"What don't you get Jordan? He loves Katie. How am I supposed to deal with that?"

"I don't believe he loves her. Maybe he's getting nostalgic, but Drew is in love with you and all of your crazy," he said, motioning at him with his hand like I was a mess.

Okay, I guess I *was* a mess at that moment, but still!

I glared at Jordan, "Great, so you think I'm crazy? I suppose you think I need therapy, too?"

Jordan shook his head, "Cami, stop. Drew told me he suggested you both go to therapy, which is not an uncommon or a horrible thing, you know?"

"Right. I'm sure you'd be thrilled if Haley suggested you went to therapy."

Jordan sighed, "She kind of did suggest that once before Aylin was born. She told me I was running from my past. It hurt, but I listened... eventually."

"Jordan, I'm not going back home. I took time off to go to that stupid reunion with him, and I felt like a complete idiot. It's not all me that's been acting weird. He can come to me if he wants to fix us."

"Fine," Jordan said, knowing I wasn't going to budge.

"You have to be at the radio station in twenty minutes," I ordered before walking out.

"I don't know how you fucking worry about work even when your world is upside down," Jordan said in disbelief.

I turned to him and wiped my eyes.

"Because work is the only thing I have control over. It's the only thing that never let me down."

Jordan sighed, "Don't count my brother out just yet."

I went back to Danny's room and sat down on the couch with my phone. Ben was watching cartoons while Danny fixed his hair in the bathroom. I turned my phone on and listened to my voicemail.

There was no long, drawn out messages from Drew pouring his heart out. Just one short message simply saying, "Call me." I would have felt somewhat better if an "I love you" plea was thrown in at the end.

I decided I wasn't open to speaking with Drew right then. In fact, I wasn't open to speaking to anyone about my relationship either. I just wanted to immerse myself into work, my son and Tortured—it was how I always survived. Tomorrow I would face Drew and any possibility of my world crumbling.

A little while later, Danny and I were walking through Centennial Park with Ben and Tilly. Being November, the foliage was beautiful and the weather was just right; breezy, but not bitter. Ben ran around, trying to pet squirrels and birds that were too quick for him. Danny and I strolled semi-quietly watching him as Tilly sniffed patches of grass.

There was a bench and I sat down, Tilly immediately lay at my feet—well, on my feet, but she had come a long way with her space invasion.

"Jordan says she's better behaved when you're around," Danny smirked.

"Maybe she's scared of me," I shrugged.

Danny laughed, "Maybe, but I think she loves you."

I smiled, "I can use all the love I can get."

He brushed my hair back from my shoulder and I looked over at him.

"I love you."

I swallowed, "I know."

"No matter what happens, please know you are loved. By me, by Drew, and even by Jordan."

I laughed, "I really do come off that insecure, huh?"

I wanted to disappear. How did this happen to me? How did I, Cami Woods, become so fragile and desperate for love?

"I wasn't trying to offend you, but I know that us three—aside from Ben," he said, nodding over to our son who was running toward us. "We're the men you've cared for most."

I nodded just as Ben ran into my arms. I squeezed him and he sat on the ground to play with Tilly. I looked over at Danny and reached out to touch his face. He is such a good-looking man—loveable and devilish all at once.

I leaned over and kissed his jawline softly, holding my hand to his cheek. He looked into my eyes and he knew I wouldn't object at that moment as his lips moved closer to mine. We kissed lightly, almost friendly, until Danny's tongue found its way into my mouth. I pulled away after a moment, remembering where we were, who we were with, and what this could mean.

I am, after all, still engaged to Andrew Ashton. I wanted to keep it that way, but lord knows what he was doing or was planning to do with Miss Katie Lawson.

"Sorry," Danny said.

"It's okay," I told him. "We should go."

As I watched the show at Bridgestone Arena, holding Ben in my lap, my mind drifted back in time. I was so reluctant to feel anything for Drew—so afraid to truly fall in love, knowing how much Danny hurt me, and how my love for him was not true. I couldn't imagine the feelings being deep and having my heart broken. I was terrified of the pain I was now beginning to feel.

How can one person give me such happiness and rip it away?

"Mama, are you crying?"

I looked down at Ben and he was staring at me; his adorable little face concerned. I tried to wipe my tears.

"Do you miss Drew?"

I nodded and Ben hugged me. I couldn't help but sob into my four-year-old's tiny shoulder while "Haley's Letter" played in the background.

After the show, Sebastian suggested we all go out for a late night dinner. I passed and explained I needed to get Ben to bed.

"I can stay with him," the tour assistant offered as she overheard.

"Thank you, but honestly, I just want to go back to the hotel."

The guys all looked at me.

"Are you sure?" Jordan asked.

I nodded and told them goodbye, but Danny stopped me.

"I'll come with you."

I didn't argue, but I could see the anger on Jordan's face. I honestly didn't know what would happen once we put Ben to bed. Would Danny make a move on me? Would I allow it? I thought about how much it hurt to be cheated on, and even if Drew was doing it to me, I knew I couldn't do it to him.

Danny carried Ben, who was already falling asleep, to an awaiting car.

"Have I ever told you how great of a dad you are?" I asked.

He smiled at me, "Why do I feel like this compliment is leading to a letdown?"

I laughed, "You know me too well."

"I do and I know you feel guilty about the kiss."

I swallowed, "It was really nice and I meant it when I said I love you..."

"But you're in love with Drew and you're engaged to him," Danny said, almost like he was reminding us both why the kiss was wrong.

"I don't know what's going to happen with Drew and me, but you deserve to be a first choice," I said, delicately.

Danny pressed his face into Ben, who was now sleeping with his mouth open on his shoulder.

"I'm sorry."

He looked over at me, "Don't be sorry. Karma is a bitch. I had you and I screwed you over. I just want you to be happy, Cami."

I smiled, "I hope I can allow myself to be."

"Me too. Just give Drew a chance to explain."

I nodded, suddenly wanting nothing more than to call Drew and allow him to tell me his side of things. I imagined him telling me how crazy I was to think he could want to be with anyone but me.

When we made it up to Danny's room, I was ecstatic to see Drew standing there. He looked exhausted and I hoped he was just as distraught as I was about what happened yesterday.

Danny nodded at Drew.

"What's up?"

Drew didn't respond. He basically stared Danny down as he opened the door.

"I'm really happy you're here," I said, hurrying toward Drew.

He kept his hands in his jacket pockets as I wrapped my arms around him. He felt like stone as I tried to hug him.

"Where can we go to talk?"

"There's a conference room that we can probably use. Or we can get a room for the night," I said.

"I don't think I'm staying the night."

I stared at him, trying to read his face.

"Oh. You have to get back to Katie, huh?" I crossed my arms over my chest.

He shook his head, "Fuck you, Cami."

"Fuck me? You already did that, Drew."

"Oh yeah? How did I do that? I was not the one who ran out of my reunion like a spoiled brat, and made a public scene for all of the tabloids!"

"Who cares about the tabloids?!" I yelled. "You never did!"

"I was never the asshole fiancé in the tabloids before. You, of course, are the victim once more."

"Do you think I like being the victim?!" I yelled.

It was obvious we were going to have this out right there in the hallway.

"I don't know, do you? You threw yourself into that spot without ever letting me explain a damn thing!"

"What am I supposed to think, Andrew?"

I never call him Andrew, but I felt a full name was needed.

"You lied about seeing your ex-girlfriend," I said, the hurt coming through. "And emailing her?" I questioned.

"I did lie," he said softly. "I was afraid of a reaction like this. I was afraid you'd want to come with me because you don't trust me."

I narrowed my eyes at him, "I do trust you."

He laughed, "If you trusted me, you wouldn't have blown up the way you did.

You wouldn't come up with every possible problem to complicate our relationship!"

"I proposed, Drew, remember?"

"Yes, and threw that in my face, remember?"

I sighed. I didn't know what to say. I just wanted to go back to the day I proposed. I wanted to erase all of these conversations we've had that hurt feelings and made us question everything.

"What happened between you and Katie the other night?"

Drew groaned, "What happened between you and Danny last night?"

"Nothing!" I yelled.

"But you slept in the same room?"

I looked down. I was a terrible liar. How was I going to deny anything? Reluctantly, I nodded.

"Same bed?"

I just looked into his eyes and he knew the answer.

"Fuck, Cami," he said, his voice almost cracking as he ran his hands through his hair.

"Nothing happened," I said, coming closer to him, wanting to reach out, but was stopped short by what he said next.

"Katie and I kissed."

My heart stopped for a second.

"You kissed?" I asked.

"It was just—so many emotions came up and... I'm sorry."

Tears filled my eyes and I blinked them back.

"Did you sleep together?"

"No," he shook his head.

"But you wanted to?"

His silence said it all. I turned around, not able to look at him.

"Do you still love her?"

I felt his hands on my shoulders and I shrugged him off.

"A part of me will always love her in some way."

It took everything inside of me not to fall to the ground. Before I could, the door opened and Danny stood there shirtless. I knew he was probably listening. Drew and I weren't exactly keeping our voices down.

"Are you sleeping in my room tonight, Cam?" he asked.

It was as if he was purposely trying to upset Drew. It worked. Just as I turned around, Drew shoved Danny against the wall.

"Drew, cut it out!" I yelled, trying to push him off Danny.

Like déjà vu, I caught Drew's elbow to my eye and I fell to the floor. All I saw were stars as I held my eye in pain.

"Cami?" I heard my name being said multiple times by Drew and Danny.

"I can't believe this happened again!" I grunted.

The last time I tried to break up a fight between Drew and Danny, I caught a punch to the ribs and was rushed to the hospital.

"Stop getting involved then," Drew hissed.

"Stop being a jackass!" I yelled back.

"Tell your ex-husband to stop causing problems in our relationship!" Drew yelled as I squinted, which only left me dizzy.

"Can you just leave Drew?"

"Let me see your eye," he sighed, trying to move my hand. "Shit, you need ice."

"What the hell happened?" I heard Jordan's voice.

I now had six men standing over me while I tried to focus my vision and process what the hell was happening to Drew and me.

A few minutes later, I was sitting in Jordan's room with an ice pack on my eye. It was just Drew and me in the room, but neither one of us were talking.

"Let me see your eye," he ordered.

I removed the pack and looked up at him.

He winced, "I'm sorry."

"For the punch or for the kiss? Or for being in love with someone else?"

He sighed, "I'm not in love with Katie. I'm in love with you."

"But you're questioning that?"

"Honestly?" he asked with his hands on his hips.

I nodded.

"Yes."

"Wow," I said, now feeling my heart throbbing as much as my eye.

"You've been acting crazy, Cami," he explained. "You didn't trust me."

"Uh, with good reason! You snuck off with Katie and kissed her."

"Maybe I wouldn't have… if we… if I didn't feel so insecure with you."

My mouth dropped, "I make you feel insecure?"

"You're so tough all the time. Sometimes it's intimidating. You have your career, all of these guys who trip over themselves to make you happy, and this great kid with a guy you're still close to... and with me, you're so quick to think someone else could mean more to me than you."

"Come here," I sighed, and patted the spot next to me. "I'm sorry if I come off too independent. I'm just used to being that way. But as much as guys trip over themselves to keep me happy—mostly because they're scared of me—you are the only guy who's ever made me truly happy," I said, lacing my fingers through his.

He smiled and kissed my eye softly.

"You're right about therapy—I think I do need it. I'm severely insecure. Even though I am super upset about you kissing Katie, I understand. Danny and I... we kissed this afternoon."

I felt Drew tense next to me.

"Don't go crazy. It didn't make me feel better. It made me miss you. It made me realize that no matter how close Danny and I remain, we will never be you and me.

Even if you and I never have a child, we will always have something so amazing and special," I explained.

Drew just listened, but I could tell he was hurt. We were both hurt and disappointed in each other. I knew what he was going to say, and though we might need it, I was so afraid we'd lose what we have, and that marriage was now out of the question.

"Cami, I think we should take some time apart."

The words came out of Drew's mouth just like I knew they would. I wanted so badly to object, but I agreed with him. I needed to get myself together.

"I think so too," I swallowed as tears streamed down my face.

But honestly, I didn't *want* to take time apart. I was afraid right then, if we didn't do it, we'd hurt each other further with bitter words and actions though.

He ran a hand through my hair and kissed me, like he was saying goodbye. He was, at least for now.

"When will we talk?" I wondered.

"I don't know," he said before standing up.

He looked at me and I could only imagine I was an awful sight—black-eyed and hysterical.

"I love you," I said.

"Love you," he nodded before walking out of the room.

I curled up on the bed and cried until Jordan came in about ten minutes later. I sat up quickly and he offered me a sympathetic look. I just walked past him and headed to Danny's room.

"I'll sleep on the couch," Danny offered and I nodded.

I was numb and no one knew what to say to me. I lay in bed, cuddling Ben close that night, and hoped it wasn't over. I knew if Drew and I didn't take some time away, we would just keep on with the petty fighting and insecure behaviors. I may lose him anyway if he decides to pursue Katie in our time apart, but at least this way, we won't have to pretend we're not drowning each other with our doubts.

Chapter Nine

"Mama, are you okay?"

I was kneeling over the toilet, feeling anything but okay.

"I'm fine, baby boy," I called back to Ben before hurling once more.

It had been a week since that night and aside from feeling heartbroken, I've had three puking episodes that were spaced out enough to lead me to purchase another pregnancy test that morning. I had never taken the first one I bought while I was in New York.

As I waited for the results, I had another vomiting episode. I picked myself up off the ground and brushed my teeth before daring to peek over at the test, which revealed a vibrant plus sign.

All at once, several emotions rushed at me. The first? Elation. I loved being a mother and was excited to give Ben a sibling. On top of that, I wanted nothing more than to be able to share such a blessing with Drew. However, when I thought of Drew, I wondered if he wanted a child with me simply to compete with Danny or to hold onto us. I had no doubt that he would be an amazing father, but I also didn't want to use a baby to hold onto a man. I knew that would never work.

I wrapped the test in toilet paper and tossed it in the trash, deciding it was best to keep the results to myself until Drew and I at least saw each other again. We haven't even texted yet, which killed me. I didn't know where he was; who he was with, or if he was as miserable as I was without him.

"Your boo-boo makes your tummy hurt," Ben said when I got out of the bathroom.

I had to laugh that he thought the black eye, which was now faded, was making me vomit.

"Give me a kiss," I said, kneeling down to him.

Ben kissed my lips and hugged me tight. "Oh, I feel better already."

We left the room a moment later and I dropped Ben off to Danny.

"Your eye is looking much better," he told me.

"Yeah, I won't have to wear my sunglasses indoors finally," I rolled my eyes.

"Have you heard from him?"

I shook my head and he squeezed my neck soothingly.

"Maybe you should call him or send him a text."

I sighed, "He wants space, D. Anyway, I have to go. I'll see you later."

I kissed Ben goodbye and met up with Haley in the hotel lobby. She thought it would be fun to have a girls' day together with Tasha, who was late of course. Tasha was usually running late. When she finally made it down to the lobby, my stomach was growling.

"Sorry, Sebastian was being difficult," Tasha laughed, her curly hair moving with the vibration.

Sebastian always teased Tasha about going out without him and looking too good. Tasha ate it up with a spoon, of course.

A little while later, but not soon enough for me, we were seated at Gracias Madre, a vegan hot spot in West Hollywood—Haley's choice, obviously. This place served fancy iced tea that looked like cocktails and offered al fresco seating where reality stars sat with dark sunglasses on, hoping to be noticed. The food was always good, though, so I never argued when she wanted to go while we're in town together.

I crunched on tortilla chips as we all perused the menu. Tasha didn't touch the chips, mentioning something about wanting to save calories for dessert. She was good at balancing. While she kept her dancer physique, she always indulged when she wanted to. She kept a healthy, curvaceous figure that men drooled over and insecure women scoffed at. I used to be one of those women, but with age, and after giving Tasha a real chance, I've grown to like her rather than try to chop her down to make myself feel better.

"So what are you and Seb doing for Thanksgiving?" Haley asked.

"My parents want us to sail to The Bahamas on their boat," she shrugged, unenthusiastically.

"Oh, poor you," I chuckled.

"It would be nice and all, but the band has less than a week off. I kind of want to just be at home together."

"I know what you mean," Haley nodded.

"You guys going to your parents' cabin?" I asked Haley.

"My parents are actually going to Europe for the holiday, for a change. We're thinking of just staying home. You guys are all welcome to come," she smiled.

"Thanks, I'll let you know," Tasha said.

I decided to immerse myself back into the tortilla chips to escape answering.

"Cami?"

"Huh?" I asked, my mouth full.

"Thanksgiving dinner? You and Ben?"

"Um, I don't know. I might go to Staten Island to see Danny's mom."

"Danny said his mom was staying with him in the City for the holiday," Tasha intervened.

"Oh, perfect," Haley smiled. "Then you can all come over."

"What about Drew?" I asked.

"What about him?"

"Is he coming?"

"Most likely," Haley shrugged.

"I don't know if he'll want to see Danny... or me."

Haley and Tasha collectively sighed.

"You still live together, Cami," Tasha said. "I think you can handle Thanksgiving together."

"Maybe he'll be spending it with Katie," I offered.

"Oh please," Haley waved me off. "I'm sure Drew misses you like crazy and hasn't even seen Katie since the reunion."

"Haley, you live in a fairytale world. I don't know where Drew's head is, and he is obviously bothered by my relationship with Danny, so I think I will pass at being the big family you want us to be on Thanksgiving," I said, in a rather snippy tone.

"Cami—"

"Hay, just let it go," Tasha mumbled.

"Where is the waitress? I'm starving," I sighed.

"Have some more chips," Haley said, but when she glanced into the basket it was empty.

I looked at her sheepishly, "Told you I'm starving."

The waitress came over just then, like she was waiting for the perfect moment to help change the topic of conversation. I was grateful. I rather not speak about Drew to anyone at the moment. I wanted to talk to him, not about him. I especially wanted to avoid the topic of him now knowing I am pregnant.

There was so much to think about with this baby. Aside from the fact that the kid's father might be falling back into love with his old girlfriend, I need to do everything in my power to make sure I have a smooth pregnancy. I had a stressful pregnancy with Ben, and I'm not getting any younger.

"How's Aylin?" I asked, after we ordered.

"Still hanging out with Rad," Haley sighed.

I laughed, "She's a good girl, Hay. She knows right from wrong, besides they're just friends."

"I know," Haley nodded. "I just hate seeing her in the tabloids next to him. I don't want her to be wrapped up in his drama. Jordan and I have tried so hard to keep her out of the spotlight so she can be normal."

Tasha interrupted, "Haley, what is normal? Did either of us live what is considered a normal life? Cami, did you?"

I shook my head, "Definitely not. Haley, being around musicians, like the band, and artist-types, like you and Tasha, is normal for Aylin. She has fun with Rad, and as far as I know, he's clean now. Besides, Aylin is super smart. She knows a bad scene and when to get out."

While I wasn't initially supportive of Aylin befriending Rad Trick, I did think she was a good influence on him. From what she's told me, he's been really sweet to her.

Haley smiled, "I know. I'm still her mother and I can't keep an eye on her like I used to now that she's in college. It's hard for me." She then laughed. "Was this what my parents felt?"

"Your parents took it to the extreme for sure," Tasha assured her.

"Speaking of parents," Haley said, pushing her hair behind her ears. "Chuck Ashton is coming for Thanksgiving."

I groaned, "I'm really not coming then."

Drew and Jordan's father was my least favorite person. No one really liked him, but we tolerated him on occasion because he pretty much had no one but his sons. I sometimes think Jordan wouldn't even keep in touch with Chuck if it weren't for Haley's bleeding heart.

"Oh my God, Tami, is that you?"

I looked up and saw a whole lot of sun and a person blocking it. All I could make out was blue hair. That combined with the goof on my name, I knew it could only be one person.

"Topaz, hi," I said.

Topaz was a pop singer who pretty much bought her way into the industry. She wasn't that great of a singer, but she was very good at marketing herself and putting on an outrageous stage show. She was Drew's tabloid-only girlfriend for a bit, but has really been dating one of his teammates, Will Nostri, on and off for the past few years.

"I just saw Drew and was asking how you were."

Like he would know, I wanted to say. Instead, I couldn't stop myself from wondering where she saw him... and who he was with.

"Oh really? Where was this?"

"A few of the guys on the team got together for dinner. The wives and girlfriends were invited too. I was surprised you weren't there."

"I'm on tour with Tortured right now," I explained, motioning to Haley and Tasha.

Topaz looked confused as she looked at them, as if to say, "There are no women in that band". It then clicked.

"Oh, I've seen you both before, hi," she waved at them. "Anyway, Drew must be really bummed, huh?"

I looked at her blankly. Did he tell her about us?

"Um, about?"

"Well, about missing the World Series. I mean—the Yankees probably would have won if Drew were playing. Will always says how Drew's energy makes everyone play their best."

I smiled sadly at that. Drew's energy not only made his team play better, but it made everyone happier. I missed that—being around him, feeding off that energy. He has been down ever since the injury and I don't think he wanted to admit how much missing the World Series affected him. This would have been the third time he got to play in the World Series, but the Yankees never won the pennant while Drew was on the team.

"Yeah, he's a great motivator."

"I just hope he's not beating himself up. He wasn't himself at dinner. I bet he misses you too. I mean, everyone had a date, but him."

I really wanted to bolt out of there and jump on the next plane to New York. Topaz made Drew sound like a sad, lost puppy that needed me to hold him. I wanted to do that for him, but I couldn't just pretend that nothing had changed. He had feelings for someone else! As for me, I was carrying our child and didn't know if telling him would put us in a pretend world.

We'd stay together and get married for the kid's sake, only for him to resent me, or have an affair behind my back. I couldn't live like that, not again. I had wondered if I loved Drew enough, if I would break his heart because I didn't trust enough in love—none of that is a question for me anymore.

I love Drew more than I could process because in spite of whatever is going on with him and Katie—I want him to be happy. I want to see him light up again, for his team, for himself, for the world—even if I'm not completely in that world. If I am not who he truly wants, which kills me inside to think like that, I can't trap him with our child.

Before I could control what was happening to me at the table, staring up at

Topaz, I found myself bolting for the bathroom, knowing tears were streaming down my face, and everyone had seen. I vaguely could hear Topaz ask if I was okay.

I didn't hold back once I was in the bathroom. The pain in my chest at the thought of losing Drew was unbearable. I just let it all out in angry and sad sobs. I slammed my fist into the hand dryer, which was stupid because it really hurt.

By the time Haley found me, make-up was all over my face and my hand was bleeding.

"Cami," she let my name escape her lips in a gasp.

I could tell she didn't know what to do with me.

"I'm okay," I lied, but it came out in hiccups.

"No, you're not. You need to just see Drew and talk."

"He doesn't want to see me," I said, my throat constricting.

"He never said that. He said time apart, but look at you," she said as I began washing the blood off my fist. "You're out here on the road when you just want to be with him. I know he misses you."

"He told you that?"

"Yes," Haley said, like I was crazy not to know that. "He misses you and Ben, and he's terribly lonely in the penthouse. You need to go home. You know Sebastian and Jordan can handle whatever business needs to be taken care of. Danny has Ben, just go."

I nodded, turning off the water and grabbing a paper towel to wipe my face.

"Can I finish lunch first?" I asked.

She laughed, "Sure."

Chapter Ten

Danny and Ben watched me pack.

"So, I'll see you guys in a few days, okay?"

Ben pouted, "Mama, what about Thanksgiving?"

I turned and smiled at him, "Would I miss a holiday with you? You and Daddy will be home in a few days and we'll spend it as one big, happy family."

"Drew, too?" Ben asked, his eyes wide and bright.

"Drew, too," I smiled, hoping I wasn't lying to my son.

I looked at Danny's face, not sure what to make of his expression. Lately, I hurt for everyone. For myself, obviously. For Drew—his torn feelings, him feeling like he let the team down, like he let me down. For Jordan and Haley—being in an awkward position with Drew and me. For Danny, with whatever he was feeling for me and his loneliness and jealousy. I even felt a bit sorry for Rad Trick and his unrequited crush on Aylin.

The hormones of this pregnancy were surely going to kill me, but I also realized Drew was right—a therapist couldn't hurt. My heart was broken at a young age; not by Danny, or Jordan, but by my father for leaving, and then my mother for dying and leaving me alone to fend for myself. I never fully dealt with any of that, and now, at forty years old, it was all trying to swallow me up.

Drew and I had plenty to sort through, our jealousy and insecurities being at the top of the list before we could move forward with marriage. I want to do things right with him, not rush into bigger commitments without fully dealing with what wasn't working in our relationship. That was how I ended up divorced in the first place.

"Are you going to call Drew and let him know you're coming?" Danny asked.

"I thought about it, but I'm afraid he'll tell me not to."

"Listen," he said, taking Ben off his lap and standing up. "I know I haven't been yours and Drew's biggest supporter, but seeing you hurt like this," he sighed. "I know how much you love him."

Just hearing Danny say those words forced tears to pour out and my lower lip began to tremble.

"Jesus, I didn't mean to make you cry," he laughed.

"I'm hormonal," I waved him off.

"Are you sure you're not pregnant? That's the only time I've seen you this easy to tears."

I didn't respond and Danny stared at me.

"You're pregnant?"

I nodded, wiping my tears and trying to smile. It must have looked ugly. Danny fought a smirk as he stood up and hugged me.

"Congratulations," he whispered.

"Thanks," I sobbed harder, burying my head into his chest.

"Cami, Drew is going to be thrilled. This is what he wanted."

I didn't say it aloud, but all I could think of was: what if Drew didn't want any of this with me now? Katie would make the perfect mom and wife. She taught Drew how to cook and was an elementary school teacher—the girl next door. They could move to the suburbs and have the perfect life.

With me, I was a city girl, always on the go. My work didn't always end at the office, and I liked to be spontaneous and change plans last minute. As a mom, I thought I did a pretty good job, but my son was on the road half the time with his father or me. Some people might think that was no way to raise a child.

There was a knock at the door and Danny pulled out of the hug to open it. Tilly came barreling in and I wrapped my arms around her furry neck, hugging her tightly and surprising everyone.

"Cami, is that you?" Jordan teased me about my sudden outburst of affection with the dog.

I wiped my face and stood up.

"You know we'll see you in a few days, right?" he joked about my tears.

I know the band was not used to seeing me emotional. I think it made them uncomfortable.

"Mama's hormel, Uncle J," Ben told him.

"Hormel?" Jordan questioned. "Like the chili?"

Ben shrugged, "I guess."

I had to laugh and so did everyone else. Jordan pulled me into a hug.

"Tell my brother I said hi. I didn't mention anything to him that you were coming. I figured you'd want it to be a surprise."

I smiled, "Thanks. Hopefully, it'll be a good surprise."

"It will be. He asks about you every time we text or talk."

That made me feel good. I finished my goodbyes before heading out of the hotel.

Unfortunately, the five-hour flight to New York was not such a great one for me. I threw up twice and had a pounding headache. I finally fell asleep about three hours in and woke up with a stiff neck. It was almost midnight by the time I landed in New York.

I took a taxi to the penthouse and felt incredibly relieved and elated to be home. I walked into the building and greeted the doorman, Gary, sleepily before making my way to the elevator. It felt like the thing took forever to come down and then seemed agonizingly slow climbing up to the top floor.

I put my key into the door and my heart pounded with the anticipation of seeing

Drew. I opened the door and all of the lights were out. I flipped the switch in the hallway before making my way to the bedroom.

I took off my coat and kicked my shoes off.

"Drew?" I called out. Nothing.

I walked into the kitchen and checked the calendar on the wall. His schedule was clear according to it. Maybe he just went out. I waited up for an hour before I just climbed into bed. Sleep didn't come, though. Panic struck me. What if something happened to him? I sat up and turned on the bedside lamp.

I grabbed my phone and called him, not caring what time it was, or who he maybe was with...

While the phone rang, the who part, more than the where of it all, hit me hard. What if he was with Katie? What if he was with any girl? I felt like such an idiot. Just as I was about to hang up, the line picked up. It wasn't Drew who answered, but it wasn't a girl either.

"Cami?" a whispered, tired voice answered.

"Matt?!" I almost shouted.

"That was my ear," he chuckled. "Hold on," he said.

I waited quite curiously, wondering how my friend, Matt Porter, who should be in Tampa, was answering Drew's phone.

When he came back on the line, he spoke a little louder.

"What's up?"

He acted as if I was calling him to make small talk at one a.m.!

"Um, just wondering where Drew is."

"Oh, he's with me."

"Duh, I figured that out already. Where is he exactly?"

"Passed out on my couch. We were playing videogames and drank a little too much, and I woke up to his phone ringing while he just snored away," he laughed.

"So, he's in Tampa with you?"

"Yes. Where are you?"

"New York, at our place!" I huffed.

"He didn't know you were coming?"

"No, it was a last minute thing and I wanted to surprise him."

Matt chuckled, "That's kind of cute. Want me to wake him?"

"No," I sighed. "How is he?"

"Drunk."

"Matt," I groaned.

"He misses you. What do you think?"

"I don't know what to think."

"Come out here and see him."

"I don't know."

"It's your call. He's coming back for Thanksgiving. Maddie misses you. She keeps asking Drew where you are."

As much as I wanted to see Drew, it seemed silly to fly out to Florida when he would be home in two days. I told Matt I'd sleep on it before I headed back to bed.

When I woke up, all that was on my mind was going to Tampa—to be with Drew in the same environment we fell for each other in. I missed his house there. I missed Matt and Laura—and not to mention their little girl, Maddie. I went into our home office to look up flights on the laptop. A picture of Drew and I kissing sat on the desk and I smiled. It was my favorite picture of us.

It was Old-Timers' Day at Yankee Stadium and Drew brought me to meet so many of the players I grew up watching play. It meant a lot to me. The photo was taken by a photographer for YES! Network. Drew was in his pinstripe home uniform and was wearing his cap backwards—which I loved. I was wearing a navy Yankees tank top and a pinstripe skirt with my arms wrapped around Drew as we made out like no one was watching. You can see the love and passion for each other in that picture. Looking at it made me want to get to Tampa quicker.

When I woke the computer from hibernation mode—Drew always forgot to shut it down—his email inbox was on the screen. It only took a second to register what I was seeing—an email thread between him and Katie.

She had initiated the series of emails and they dated back to before the reunion. I knew I probably shouldn't read his email, but I was too curious.

From: misskatielawson@nj.edu
To: DrewAshton12@mlb.com
Subject: hi :-)

Hi Drew,

I wanted to reach out to you. Are you coming to our college reunion? It would be really nice to see you...

I've been thinking a lot about us and how terrible it was of me to reject your proposal all those years ago. Even more so, I'm ashamed of the reason why. I knew what your dream was when I met you, and yet, I somehow expected you to give it up for me.

I'm sorry. I just loved you so much that I didn't want to share you with the Yankees. I didn't want that kind of life for our children or me. I used to dream of having your babies.

Anyway, I had gotten married to everything I thought I wanted. A 9 to 5 guy who treated me well, but I didn't love him—not like I loved you. I miss you and think about you often. I'm sorry for doing this by email, but it's the only way I could contact you. Your number has changed since college, I would imagine.

I know you're with someone now, and I'm completely out of line. I just needed you to know... I will always love you, and I'm sorry I hurt you.

Love always,
Your Lady Katie

After reading Katie's pouring her heart out apology, I wanted to knock her teeth out. How dare she go after my man?! At the same time, if I were her, I'd feel like I screwed up too. Still, I would never like her. Heartbreaker. Man stealer. Bitch.

I swallowed, not really wanting to read Drew's reply, but not being able to stop myself.

Hey Katie,

Wow. I don't know how to respond to that. Not by email anyway. Maybe we can get together, before the reunion preferably. Here's my number, give me a call or text me.

I miss you too and I understand you were trying to protect yourself. You should know though, I love my fiancée very much, and have no intentions of screwing anything up with her.

Drew

I let out a deep breath. I felt relieved, but knew his intentions weren't good enough since obviously things changed when he saw her again.

The next couple of emails discussed everyday things, like the school Katie worked at, where she lived in New Jersey, as well as Drew's traveling, Jordan, and his injury. He did mention me, too, much to my surprise and delight. He would talk about missing me, how busy I was with my career, and how he loved that about me, but wished he had more time with me. And he spoke about Ben, and how much he loved him, and hopes to someday have a kid of his own. I smiled, overjoyed that Drew spent so much time telling Katie about my son and me.

One of the last emails was the night before we took a break. This time, Drew started it.

I don't know what I'm doing anymore. I'm so confused and angry with myself. I never wanted to hurt Cami, and I did. I love her, Katie. That's not to say I didn't feel nostalgic seeing you again, but we can't just erase the past ten years. You hurt me and I moved on. I'm so angry that you are back now, expecting me to what... leave the life I have with Cami? With the Yankees? I can't just walk away.

Cami gets my career—loves me for it, not in spite of it. She's a strong, independent woman, and sometimes that can be intimidating, but I admire her for who she is and all that she's accomplished. She's amazing, and I'm not saying that to hurt you, but you need to know how I feel about her.

I don't think spending time with you right now is a good idea. I just need time and space from everything. Please allow that.

My heart rate returned to normal. I felt a huge sense of relief. I am still surprised that Drew could be intimidated by me. He never showed it or expressed it until more recently.

I knew going to Florida to see him would not be the right decision. He obviously went there to clear his head, not to have me show up.

I wanted so badly to just be mad at him, but I couldn't. I understood how he felt. I had feelings for Jordan for so long and I couldn't control them. I never thought I would get over him, but then Drew stole my heart, and ever since then, I didn't want anyone else.

I grabbed my cell phone and went into my text messages. I opened a thread of messages between "Hot Ass" and me. I had changed Drew's name in my phone to "Hot Ass" when we first began hooking up. I was paranoid someone would find out—like Jordan—and he would totally hate me for fooling around with his little brother. Plus, Drew has the hottest butt I've ever seen, or felt. I missed it. I missed him. The last time he had texted me was the night of his reunion.

Please talk to me, Cami. I love you.

My chest hurt thinking about him. I typed three words and contemplated sending them or not.

I need you.

I had never felt such a yearning before. I grew up knowing I couldn't depend on anyone. I grew up alone, understanding I had to look out for myself and guard my heart. Needing someone, especially a man, only led to bad things. That was what I learned from my mother.

Did I really *need* Drew? Was it okay to need someone? I don't know anymore, but I sure felt like I needed him. At the very least, I wanted him—here. Now. Always.

I deleted the message before I could send it. Whether I needed Drew or not, I didn't think telling him that right then was smart. I could have already lost him, and being clingy and needy might be the nail in the coffin. After all, I already intimidated him!

...

After pulling myself together somewhat, I decided to pamper myself while I had time alone. I spent the day at a spa. A massage was just what the baby and I needed after all of the emotions we've been through and traveling we've done.

Afterward, I sat in Central Park, enjoying the fall weather and thinking about the baby. It was therapeutic, not worrying about my relationship with Drew or Danny or business. I just thought about Ben being a big brother and if the little one would be a girl or boy.

I allowed all those warm feelings of being a mom comfort me. Motherhood had definitely changed me for the better; it made me more compassionate and happier. I began to think of my own mother—who spent her life providing for me, even though we never had much. She worked so incredibly hard that she didn't have much time for anything else—even giving me the attention I needed. It sounded so familiar. Sure, I wasn't slaving away on my feet nonstop, but I tended to throw myself into work more often than not.

I had gotten better over the years, but still, I felt the need to involve myself in every aspect of my business—even if I'm not needed. I was a control freak and I did love my work, but I found myself more stressed trying to balance it all lately.

I took a deep breath and called Colin. He was practically my right hand guy at Out of the Woods Entertainment. I relied on him more than anyone else.

"Hello love, how's the tour going?" His Irish accent had mellowed out some over the years.

"Great. I'm home actually."

"Oh, checking up on us here?"

"No. Actually, I wanted to talk to you about something."

"Shoot," he said, but I could hear the worry in his voice.

Usually when I began a conversation this way, it meant I was annoyed.

"Can you meet me for dinner?"

"Won't Drew be jealous?" he chuckled.

"I'm not hitting on you. This is about business."

After I hung up with Colin, I headed back home. I sat in the home office, searching for a therapist that maybe Drew and I could see together. I found one who specialized in relationships, family and parental issues. I wanted to fight for Drew— to let him know how much he meant to me and that I was willing to work on myself.

Am I still hurt and mad about Katie? Of course, but I know Drew wasn't trying to hurt me, or even cheat on me. I mean, all he and Katie did was kiss. I hope that was still true. How could I not forgive him when I kissed Danny? Someone who *had* to be in my life constantly. All things considered, Drew handled my relationship with my ex-husband better than anyone I know.

Dinner that night with Colin went well. He caught me up on things at the office. I caught him up on things with Tortured.

"So, I want to step back from work."

Colin looked at me wide-eyed.

"For a few months, like when Ben was a baby?" he asked.

I shook my head, "No. Indefinitely. Maybe permanently."

Colin laughed, "Good one, Cami."

"Seriously. I want to be there for Ben. I want to be there when he gets home from school. I want to be able to travel with Drew. I want to visit my favorite band, Tortured, on the road, not as their manager, but as their friend."

Colin stared at me blankly.

"Can you do that?"

"Honestly, probably not," I had to laugh. "Look, I still want to own Out of the Woods. I still want to be involved in signing new acts, in helping with the direction of careers, but as far as the day-to-day involvement of the company..." I shook my head. "I want you to be my COO."

Colin's mouth dropped and it took him a second to respond. I have never seen him caught so off-guard. Gone was the suave Irishman with the sneaky smile and squinty eyes. In his place was a wide-eyed, open-mouthed unsure boyish-man.

"Really?"

"You practically do the job as it is when I'm not around. Let's make it official."

"Does that mean a salary increase?"

"Of course," I nodded. "After the holiday, we'll sit down with the payroll department and work it all out. That is, if you want the position?"

"Of course I do. You know how much I love working with this company and you all of these years."

"I'm sorry I was always so hard on you. I needed to earn a lot of respect as a very young woman in the industry."

"Don't apologize," Colin put his hand up. "I wouldn't have been such a go-getter without you yelling at me to be," he laughed.

The restaurant wasn't far from my apartment, so I decided to walk home. When I got there, a redhead was standing at the front desk talking to my doorman. Her back was to me, but I had a feeling it was her.

"He's not home? Are you sure?" the redhead asked. "Do you know when he left?"

"Ma'am, I can't tell you that," Gary said before noticing me standing there. "Miss Woods," he called me over. "Maybe you know this young lady and can help."

Katie Lawson turned around and I could tell she was both shocked and embarrassed to see me standing there.

"Hi Katie," I said.

I felt like punching her, but at the same time, I kind of felt sorry for her—embarrassed for her even. Was she really trying to stalk Drew at our apartment?

"Why don't we talk?" I suggested, knowing I was nuts.

A few minutes later, we were entering the penthouse. The elevator ride had been awkwardly silent.

"Have you been here before?" I wondered as I closed the door behind her.

She shook her head as she looked around. Should I offer her a tour? Rubbing my life with Drew in her face seemed like something I wouldn't think twice about back in the day, but it just seemed awkward and villainous to show off walls of photos and the bed where we have made love.

"Drew didn't feel right about it," she assured me.

I nodded and I guess I should have been relieved, but it made me quite curious what went on between them.

"Can I get you something?"

"Why are you being nice to me?" she asked.

I swallowed, "I'm really not sure. Maybe because I feel sorry for you—that you're so down on your life that you're trying to steal mine."

"Cami," Katie tried to argue. "I don't want to steal anything from you. I just—I'm in a bad place. I just went through a really hard divorce and with the reunion…"

"You got nostalgic," I rolled my eyes.

"Drew was my first love. I never stopped loving him."

"You were the ass who let him go. You were the reason I had to be the one to propose to him, and I'm supposed to sit back and let you hurt him all over again?"

"I don't want to hurt him."

"But you did. He hasn't changed, Katie. He's still a baseball player. He's still the guy that jokes around too much. The one who loves to work out and listen to pop music really loudly."

Katie looked down at her fingernails. I could tell I burned her. Drew had once told me she used to try and change him. She'd want him to read more, listen to classical music, and be serious. Drew was intelligent, sure, but he was so much fun to be around and carefree. God, how he could turn the worst days into the best ones. I always tried to be that for him, but he was not down very often, until recently anyway. Well, I guess I didn't do so well to ease his pain.

"No, he hasn't changed, but I have," Katie sighed.

I stared at her.

"Obviously not. You're still selfish."

"Excuse me?" Katie gasped. "You don't even know me!"

"I know enough, Katie. Drew asked you to give him space and here you are at his doorstep!" I yelled.

"How do you know what Drew asked me?"

I didn't respond since I only knew from reading their emails. I wish Drew had told me these things himself, but I guess you don't tell your fiancée, who you're taking a break from, what you say in emails to ex-girlfriends. That would be like me telling

Drew what Danny and I have talked about. Well, I kind of did do that. Maybe that's where I went wrong—I was too honest with Drew about Danny's feelings for me. I could tell it bothered him. Ugh, I'm honest to a fault, and I thought that was my best trait. I guess not.

"From what I know, Drew asked for space from you too, so what are you doing here?" Katie turned on me, with an accusing tone.

This bitch doesn't know who she's dealing with!

"I fucking live here!" I yelled. "How dare you come here and try to get information about my fiancé's whereabouts. Get out!"

Katie shook her head, "Gladly!"

She opened the door and turned toward me.

"By the way, if he's your fiancé, what the hell was he doing sleeping at my place a couple of nights ago?" she smirked.

Before I could slap her, she clamped her hand over her mouth. She obviously knew she said something she shouldn't have, which made me believe it was actually true, and not just spiteful.

I shoved her hard.

"You need to leave," I said, not knowing if my temper was going to hold back anymore.

I wanted to claw her innocent-looking face and rip the fiery hair from her head. Really, her hair was a soft natural red, but somehow, all I saw was fire at that point.

"Cami, I'm sorry," Katie said, tears coming to her eyes.

I shoved her toward the door and she took the hint. After the door slammed, I found myself shaking. I just couldn't believe Drew would actually go through with sleeping with her!

I wish everyone I was close to wasn't so far away. I wanted to vent, but mostly, I wanted revenge. I knew how easy it would be to have sex with Danny, but I also knew that would only complicate things.

After all, I am pregnant with Drew's baby. Shit. Going through a divorce while pregnant was hard, but losing the love of my life while pregnant was going to destroy me.

Chapter Eleven

Matt must have told Drew about my failed surprise. He called me three times the next day until he resorted to texting. When I saw the message from "Hot Ass" pop up, I debated changing his name to just "Ass" in light of last night's visit from Katie.

Hey Cam. Trying to get a hold of you. Miss your voice. Miss your everything. I can't wait to see you. I'm hoping to get a flight home today.

I didn't reply. What would I say? "Hi Drew. Looking forward to hearing all about you sleeping with Katie!" I felt incredibly numb about the situation—like I didn't believe it. I didn't want to believe it. Katie just didn't seem like the lying type—even when she was being spiteful and territorial.

I guess I see the common thread between Katie and me now. While she seemed sweet and innocent, she was feisty and determined.

I was grateful I had things to keep me busy. I just didn't want to face any of this bullshit until I could hash it out with Drew in person. Until then, I could pretend Drew and I were getting married and had our baby on the way.

I visited my OB/GYN for my first pregnancy-related appointment. I was thankful they had a cancellation last minute. The doctor did a full examination. I was only eight weeks pregnant, which to me, wasn't far along enough to allow myself any hope. After already having a miscarriage, I knew how crucial the first trimester was for me.

"Cami, it's really important you take extreme precaution. Stress needs to stay at a minimum and so does travel."

I nodded, "I'll do my best."

On the taxi ride to the office, I rubbed my belly making a silent promise to protect my child from whatever pain I might be feeling. I walked into my office building and rounded the corner to the elevators, practically smashing into a man.

"Shit," I hissed and held my hand over my breast where the man's elbow practically shoved into me as if he were a linebacker blocking a touchdown.

"Oh hey, sorry about that," Christian Eriksson said. "Are you okay?" he asked, seeing I was rubbing my breast, and not focused at all on being cordial to him.

Part of me wanted to spite Drew and flirt with the guy who has been nothing but sugar to me. However, I knew better. I knew his suave little greetings in the elevator were all an act. I could see right through trash like Christian, even if I didn't know all of the trouble he caused my family. He was a dick of a cousin to Jordan and a slime ball of a friend to Haley as well as a controlling, lying fiancé to Tasha. Even without knowing any of that, I could see the look in his eyes and that phony smile on his face. Christian was nothing but trouble. I wouldn't be spiting Drew by being anywhere near Christian—I would be plain old stupid.

"I'm fine," I said, going to walk past him, but he grabbed my arm.

"Cami, I'm really sorry. Maybe we can grab a cup of coffee?"

I rolled my eyes, "I know all about you, Christian. If you think for one second I would go out with you—even just for a cup of coffee—you're just as delusional as everyone says you are."

He took a step back from me, but flashed me this look that sent a shiver down my spine. He just stared at me like he wanted to do something to me—slap me or kiss me—I couldn't tell, but it pretty much freaked me out. No wonder Haley was totally repulsed by him. He was cute, sure, but he had this weird, creepy element. How did Tasha ever sleep with him?

I turned away and continued onto the elevator, grateful in a few weeks, I wouldn't have to run the risk of seeing Christian every day.

My workday was filled with staff and lawyer meetings to help transition my once small company into a more structured corporation that offered some of my oldest employers and investors stake in it. It was a scary thing, allowing others control in something I built, but I felt like it was the next step—not only to make Out of the Woods Entertainment bigger, but better for me, and my employees.

At the end of it all, I felt incredibly good about my decision and about all of the time I would have with my children—and maybe Drew, that is if we can make it through what we are going through.

Could I get past him sleeping with Katie? At the moment, it hurt too damn much. However, I wanted Drew to talk to me—to hear what he was feeling, no matter how much it may hurt. Maybe I could get over it in time. That's how much I love Andrew Ashton—more than my company, more than my pride, and way more than I could ever express to him. I didn't know what it all said about me. Was I really one of those women to take a cheater back?

The thing is, Drew had been the model boyfriend the past three years, but no one is perfect—like Danny said. He may have made a mistake. Hell, I was tempted to make that same, stupid mistake with Danny. Of course, mine would have been out of spite and comfort, not a need to be with someone other than Drew. That was the part that cut the deepest. Did Drew need something from Katie that he wasn't getting from me? I hated myself for trying to take any blame, but I couldn't help but wonder where we went wrong.

On my way home, I happened to be walking to the subway station and saw a flyer from an animal shelter. Not only was I missing Drew and Ben, but I found myself missing Tilly too! I missed her cuddling and her wet nose touching my cheek. What was wrong with me? I wasn't sure, but I knew what a great welcome home present a dog would be for Ben and it would probably do me some good too.

Instead of going directly home, I took the subway to the animal shelter. I didn't know what kind of dog I was looking for, but I hoped I knew when I saw the right one.

The shelter was in the East Village, an area I hung out often in my teens and early twenties. Tortured played many shows back in the day in the area. The emo kids ate up Jordan's angst-filled lyrics with a spoon. Sometimes I missed those days, struggling to get the band's name and music out around New York City. This was the city that built me and my job was everything.

I have so much more now, and I owe a lot of it to those struggling times. I have a huge, beautiful apartment filled with memories. I have a big, loud, ridiculous family who has my back when I need them, but also put me in my place when I need that, too. I have my little boy, who I would do anything for—even get a dog for, which I would probably wind up cleaning up after all by myself. And I have Drew... no matter what happens, he's part of my family, too. Married, dating, broken up—Drew is going to be there for our child and me.

That single thought hurt me and comforted me at the same time. The thought that he would be that close to me, even if we were broken up would be torturous. To watch him move on, and bring another woman into our child's life? My heart couldn't take it. Therapy would definitely be needed.

I tried to not look like I was on the verge of crying as I entered the shelter, but crap, all of these dogs in cages were enough to make me want to take them all home. It felt like a prison, for crying out loud!

I walked up and down rows of cages. The smell was unpleasant and so was all of the whimpering. It was incredibly sad. Many of the dogs were wagging their tails and scratching at their cage dying for attention. Some were scraggly looking. Some seemed to drool an awful lot—or shed—or both. None of the dogs seemed like they could be *my* dog, in spite of my sympathy for them all. These dogs were either too small, too yappy, or too needy.

I walked up to the last cage, ready to give up on my search, when my eyes connected with the bluest of eyes I had ever seen on an animal. This dog had my mother's eyes. He was a pit bull, big and hulking, just sitting on his hind legs, panting mildly. He had a brindle coat with accents of white on his snout, chest and his huge paws.

"Hi," I said, not sure what else to say.

The dog licked his nose before standing and coming closer to me. I stuck my hand out and he sniffed it through the cage. He then tilted his head as if giving me the go ahead to pet him.

"See one you like?" A worker came over and asked me.

"How's this one with kids?" I asked as I tentatively petted the dog's head.

"Well, I'm not too sure. We found him on the street, but he's been nothing but a sweetheart."

I looked into the dog's eyes again. He looked sad.

"Most folks are too afraid to take a chance on pits and we wind up putting them down."

My heart wrenched hearing that this beautiful beast of a dog would be put down.

He licked my hand a couple of times before lying down in his cage, as if he thought I had given up on him.

Something about the dog reminded me of myself. Maybe it was the blue eyes or how intimidating he looked, or that he grew up alone. This was my dog—I knew it.

"I'll take him," I said to the man.

"You sure miss? A little thing like you with this big guy?"

"I'm sure. I'm tougher than I look."

During the taxi ride to my apartment, the pit bull paced the backseat anxiously, often stepping down on my thigh causing me to wince.

"Relax," I told him sternly.

He seemed to understand and took a seat. When we arrived at my building, I paid the driver and grabbed onto the leash before opening the door. The dog practically dragged me out of the car.

"Shit, you're strong," I whined, getting my footing and pulling tightly on the leash.

Gary opened the door for me.

"New dog Miss Woods?"

"Yup," I said, blowing a piece of hair out of my face.

"Ben will be excited I'll bet."

I smiled, "I hope so. I need his help with a name."

Once I got up to my apartment, the dog rushed inside and inspected every room before looking at me expectantly.

"What?" I asked.

He let out a small whimper and trotted over to me. He nudged my hand.

"It's okay," I said. "This is your home."

The dog's ears perked up at the word as if he understood.

"I'll get you some food in the morning."

I walked into the kitchen and he followed. I felt him watching me as I set up a bowl of water for him. My cell phone rang startling us both and I picked it up.

"Hey," Danny said.

"Hi, are you home?" I asked.

"Ben and I just landed. He's pretty cranky from jetlag. Want me to just keep him overnight and I'll bring him over in the morning?"

"Yeah. Can I talk to him?"

"Sure," Danny said.

"Hi Mama," Ben said, sounding a mixture of exhaustion and sadness with maybe a hint of anger.

"Hi baby. What's wrong?"

"I miss you," he yawned. "And I'm mad I'm tired. I don't want to be tired!" he yelled.

I heard Danny quieting him and I laughed.

"I know being tired is the worst. I miss you too. I'll see you in the morning though. And Ben, guess what? I have a surprise for you."

"What is it?!" he asked excitedly.

"You'll have to wait for tomorrow."

"Mama?"

"Yes baby?"

"Will I see Drew tomorrow? Is he my surprise?"

As if on cue, I heard a key in the front door. The dog stood in front of me protectively, but didn't growl.

"He's not the surprise, but yes, you'll see him tomorrow."

"Yes!" Ben shouted.

"Be a good boy for Daddy. I love you. Good night."

"Love you, Mama," Ben got off the phone and I wasn't thinking as I hung up the phone, barely registering Danny calling my name. Oops.

My eyes focused on Drew, who had gotten the door open. He stood in the doorway, a carry-on bag on his shoulder and rolling suitcase behind him. His hair was tousled and looked longer.

Drew's eyes settled on me before landing on the dog, who looked back at me as if he were wondering if he should attack or not. I was wondering the same thing.

"There is a dog in here," Drew said, confused.

I nodded, "He's my dog."

"What?" Drew laughed. "You got a dog? A huge dog!"

He dropped his bags and knelt down before whistling to the dog who ran over to him, tail wagging full force. The dog snuggled right into Drew and I felt like I lost the upper hand—he was not going to be *my* dog, he was going to be Drew's. Traitor.

I sighed and walked down the hall. I headed into the master bathroom and closed the door. I tied my hair into a knot on my head, thinking it was getting too long. I usually kept my hair shoulder length in the winter months and shorter in summer, but it had grown past my shoulders now. I felt my face looked too small with that much hair surrounding it. I washed the make-up off my face and brushed my teeth.

When I opened the bathroom door, Drew was laying on the bed with the dog practically on top of him.

I scoffed, "Just great."

"What?" Drew asked. "Do you not want me here?"

"I don't know what I want," I said, walking over and pulling the dog by his collar. "Down!" I ordered.

The dog whimpered, but got down from the bed immediately. As I went to my dresser to change for bed, I felt Drew wrap his arms around me from behind. He felt too good. I hated the fact that I couldn't think straight in his arms. I leaned into him and allowed his large hands to keep me pressed against him, my heart thumping beneath his palm.

"I'm sorry I wasn't here when you got home," he breathed into my hair. "I needed time away from New York and the team, and..."

"...And Katie?" I asked.

He didn't respond. I pushed him off lightly and turned to look at him.

"What happened with Katie? Please don't lie to me."

Drew nodded. He stepped back and sat on the bed, running a hand through his hair.

"I spent some time with her."

"Is that what you call it?" I sucked my teeth.

"We went out a couple of times. We kissed a couple of times..." he said, his voice thick with regret.

I tried to remain strong; to not show the ache I felt, but it was impossible. Being in love with someone was so much more of a bitch than being married to them.

Drew looked up when he could hear me crying. I was trying to be angry, not hurt, but it wasn't happening.

"Cami, I'm sorry. I didn't—Katie and I didn't sleep together. I couldn't," he said, his voice coming out breathy, like he was fighting back tears.

I stomped my foot like I was Ben throwing a tantrum.

"I'm supposed to believe that?!"

Drew stood up again and swallowed, "Yes."

"Why would Katie lie to me?" I asked, finding the anger I was searching for.

"Katie?" Drew asked. "You talked to her?"

I nodded, "Oh yeah. She had the nerve to show up here. *Here*, Drew—to our apartment!"

Drew groaned and rubbed his forehead.

"Are you kidding me? I told her to back off!" He gritted his teeth.

"Well, she loves you—did you really think that was going to happen? I hate what you did. I hate what you've put me through, and don't know what our future holds, but I was ready to fight her for you..." I said, wiping a tear. "Because love makes you stupid," I spit out. "It makes you believe that nothing can hurt you. It makes you believe that you have this perfect person who turns the bad days good."

"Cam, I never said I was perfect. And I'm sorry that Katie is being—well, Katie. I had forgotten how she was, or maybe I thought she'd change. I loved her at a point in my life, but I know I don't still love her.

The past is the past and I was wrong to dig it up," he sighed. "I'm in love with you, Cami, and the past couple of weeks have been torture."

I stared into the brown eyes I have always trusted—even if Drew didn't think I trusted him, I know deep down I did. I wasn't sure if I could still trust them now, though. The dog came over to me and nuzzled his massive head against my thigh.

"Torture?" I asked. "Sleeping with Katie was torture?"

"I didn't sleep with Katie!"

"Stop fucking lying to me!" I yelled.

Drew groaned, "I'm not fucking lying to you, Cami! You'd believe her over me? I don't know what Katie was thinking saying that to you. She was just trying to hurt you—to hurt me actually."

"Good, you deserve to get hurt," I said spitefully, though I didn't truly mean that.

No matter what Drew did to me, I couldn't bear to think of him hurt. I knew how big his heart was, even if he was a lying cheater!

"Fine, obviously you don't want to listen to the truth. I'll sleep in the guest room tonight, and we'll talk in the morning," he sighed, sounding completely exhausted.

"So, we're all heading to Jordan and Haley's tomorrow?"

"Looks like it, one big, happy family," he shot over his shoulder.

He walked to the door before turning back around.

"I've missed you, your crazy mood swings and all," he said before closing the door behind him.

My face crumbled in tears and I changed for bed. Once I got under the covers, the dog jumped in with me. I didn't have the fight to get him off and was just relieved he was still *my* dog. He practically lay on top of me—with his head on my belly—as I cried myself to sleep.

Chapter Twelve

I woke up to the dog licking my face. Ick. I mushed his face back and wiped my cheeks.

"Happy Thanksgiving, boy," I patted his head and headed into the bathroom.

I threw on some sweats and a hat before grabbing the dog's leash. I took him for a walk and managed to pick up some dog food at Aristides. I wasn't feeling great by the time I got back to the apartment.

Drew was cooking when I got in and the smell made me nauseous.

"Morning," he offered.

I waved before hurrying to the bathroom. I threw up before laying back down in bed. The dog hopped up next to me, and like last night, I didn't have the energy to kick him off. He lay his head down on my belly almost protectively. It was comforting. Drew walked into the bedroom and sat down.

He looked over at me and reached out to under my eye. He touched the healing skin softly, looking apologetic for the injury his hard-ass elbow caused. The bruise was pretty faded at this point that I almost forgot it was still there.

"Are you hungry?"

I shook my head.

"Do you want to sit with me while I eat?"

"I'm not feeling well."

"Okay," he said, getting up and walking out of the bedroom.

The dog looked over at me as if to ask when I would tell Drew about the baby. I needed to wait—at least until Drew and I decide about our relationship. I will not have him be with me out of obligation.

The doorman phone rang and I heard Drew answer it.

"Danny and Ben are on their way up!" he shouted.

"Send them in here!" I yelled back.

"Sure," Drew said loudly, followed with a quieter, sarcastic comment. "I don't mind your ex-husband in our bedroom at all."

I sighed and felt like reminding him that this bedroom was mine and Danny's first, but I figured that wouldn't help anything. After Ben was done exuberantly talking to Drew in the kitchen, he bounded into my bedroom with Danny following.

"A dog! We got a dog!" he yelled as the dog stood on the bed wagging his tail.

Danny picked Ben up and placed him on the bed. Ben and the dog were instant best friends, playing around without getting too rough. Danny patted the dog's back.

"I can't believe you got a dog," he laughed.

I shrugged as I remained laying down.

"Not feeling well?" he asked.

"Morning sickness," I said quietly.

"You still didn't tell him?"

I shook my head.

"What did you say to piss him off this morning?"

I rolled my eyes, "He's been hooking up with Katie."

Danny's jaw tightened, "I'm sorry, Cam."

I tried to force a smile as Danny leaned down and kissed my forehead.

"Mama, what's his name?" Ben asked as the dog licked his face.

"Well, I was hoping you'd name him," I smiled, running a hand through his dark brown hair.

"Hmm," Ben said, tapping his chin. "Biscuit!"

"Why Biscuit?" Danny asked as I smiled, liking the name.

"Because he's slobbery, so you need to sop him up with a biscuit!" Ben giggled.

I had to laugh too.

"Sop it up with a biscuit?" Where'd he get that?" Danny asked.

"Drew sometimes says that."

When he'd eat my tomato sauce, when he'd make biscuits and gravy, sometimes when he looked at me, Drew would say I'd look so good, he'd sop me up with a biscuit. I never realized Ben had picked up on the phrase.

"I have to start getting ready," I sighed, trying to sit up.

"I can take Ben over to Jordan and Haley's if you want."

Looking over at Ben, I knew there would be no way he was leaving Biscuit.

"It's fine. I'm sure the sickness will pass. Besides, Drew can watch Ben."

A few minutes after Danny left, Drew walked into the bedroom as I stood up, rubbing my stomach.

"You okay?" he asked.

"Fine. Can you watch Ben while I get ready?"

"Sure," he said and walked over to me.

He leaned down like he was going to kiss me, but I walked away. I didn't really want to snub him, but I didn't want to be kissed when I felt like I'd puke. I also wasn't sure if I should let Drew kiss me.

As I closed the bathroom door, I saw Ben, Drew and Biscuit playing around on my bed. I was never getting that dog out of my bed now.

A few hours later, I was buckling my seatbelt. I peeked back at Ben to make sure he was buckled.

"Is Biscuit going to be okay all alone?" Ben asked.

"Of course, he's a big boy, Ben, not a puppy," Drew said, trying to ease my son's worries.

But I was uneasy about leaving him too. Drew looked over at me and put his hand on my knee. I thought he was going to squeeze it, like he normally did, and it would make my knee jerk, but he removed his hand immediately.

I stared at him as he pulled out of the parking garage, missing his warmth—his easygoing spirit, the weightlessness I felt when he was around.

About a half hour later, we made it through the post-Thanksgiving day parade traffic and arrived at Jordan and Haley's Riverside apartment. Though apartment was hardly how it should be described. It was two floors with high ceilings and large rooms.

Aylin opened the door and wrapped her arms around her uncle first. I was surprised to see Rad Trick behind her.

"What are you doing here?" I wondered, looking between him and Aylin.

She blushed, "Um, I invited him."

"Okay," I said slowly, as I scowled at Rad.

He shrugged and opened his arms to me. Reluctantly, I hugged him.

"Relax, Cami."

"Hey Ben!" Aylin said, picking him up and hugging him.

"Aylin, we got a dog! Mama surprised me!"

"What?" Aylin asked and looked back at me.

I shrugged, "Tilly has been good to me."

As if she heard her name, Tilly came trotting up to me. I bent down and began petting her vigorously. I felt everyone staring at me.

"Who are you?" Jordan laughed, coming into the room.

"Apparently a dog lover now," Drew said.

I looked over at him and smirked, "You got that right."

He rolled his eyes and looked at Jordan, "Is Haley in the kitchen?"

"Yeah," Jordan said, and Drew headed in that direction, not even offering a hug to his brother.

"I thought you two would have made up by now."

"Don't, J," I said, standing up.

He looked at my face and pulled me into a hug.

"Happy Thanksgiving," he said.

"You too. Excuse me," I said, before hurrying to the bathroom before I could cry or throw up on him.

I took a few minutes in the bathroom, angry with myself for not being able to put on an act. I wanted to—for everyone, not just myself, but all I felt was pain. There was a knock at the door.

"Cami? It's me," Haley's voice rang through.

I opened the door and she smiled.

"Happy Thanksgiving."

"You too," I forced a smile.

"You want to talk?" She asked, coming into the bathroom and closing the door behind her.

"In here?" I had to laugh.

She shrugged, "It's not the first heart to heart we've had in a bathroom."

I rolled my eyes, "I was drunk then and feeling sorry for myself."

"And what's different now?" She teased.

"I'm sober."

"Drew told me your surprise didn't go as planned."

"The dog? Ben was surprised," I said, confused.

"You got a dog?" Haley asked.

"I missed Tilly," I said, begrudgingly.

Haley laughed, "Aw, Cami, you're nothing but a softie!"

"Tell me about it," I said, motioning to my teary face.

"The surprise I was referring to was you coming home early to see Drew..." she said.

"He was in Florida with *my* friends!" I huffed.

"Matt is just as much Drew's friend now. Besides, he went there because he was upset over you."

"Haley, Drew went to Tampa because he felt guilty for sleeping with Katie," I said, folding my arms across my chest.

She sucked her teeth, "So, you do believe that?"

"You don't?"

"No way," Haley said matter-of-factly. "Drew is not Danny. He's not a cheater and definitely not a liar."

I glared at her, "He's not a cheater?"

"Okay, so he kissed Katie a couple of times, but—"

"Haley, don't be so naïve."

"You stop being so untrusting!" She hissed. "I know my brother-in-law, and he would fess up to it if he slept with Katie," she insisted.

I blinked at her a few times.

"You believing Katie over him is really hurtful to him, Cami. If you'd just listen to him—"

"Great, so you're taking his side," I threw my hands up in the air.

"I am not taking sides! You know what? Jordan and I accepted your relationship with Drew because we actually believed you two were good for each other, but obviously, you're going to carry this on like one big drama fest like you did for twenty years with Danny!"

Was Haley yelling at me? Ugh, she didn't yell often, but when she did, it was usually extremely insightful or quite an annoying lecture. I couldn't figure out which this little speech was—maybe a mixture of the two?

"Now today is a holiday and we haven't all been together without the tour being involved in some time, so please just remember that and try to have a good time? If not for your sake or Drew's sake, then for your son's sake!"

She didn't let me respond. Haley was out of the bathroom and I had to decide whether or not I was going to continue on with my bathroom pity party of one or make the best of things.

I heard Ben telling Sebastian and Tasha about Biscuit. I could also make out Danny's and his mother's voices. The house was filling up and I was getting hungry, not having had anything to eat yet.

I fixed myself up in the mirror before walking down the hall. I greeted Sebastian and Tasha followed by Darren, who was alone, saying he and his latest girlfriend broke up, big surprise there. Haley's friend, Meghan was there with her all-too-bubbly personality. Last, but not least, Chuck Ashton had arrived in all of his bastard glory. He was talking to Drew, and I had no intention in going out of my way to say hello to him. When I got over to Danny and Leslie, I was comforted. I was always close to Leslie, even after my divorce to her son.

"How's my daughter doing?" Leslie asked, knowingly, brushing my hair behind my shoulder.

She and her son both made that gesture often. They'd sweep my hair off my shoulder, rub my back or squeeze the back of my neck. I suppose I should find it uncomfortable; something that my ex-husband and mother-in-law shouldn't be doing, but it had the opposite effect on me. It also made me wonder if they both thought my hair was too long as well.

"Been better," I shrugged.

She pulled me into a hug, "Congratulations."

She whispered the word and I thanked her, eyeing Danny.

"You know I tell her everything," he defended himself.

I nodded, "I know. I'm glad you guys know. It's been hard to celebrate these days."

"If you'd just tell him," Danny sighed.

"I want Drew to want me—just me," I explained quietly.

Danny looked at me, "How could he want anyone else?"

I laughed, "This, coming from my ex-husband who had multiple affairs."

Leslie smiled and linked an arm with mine and the other with her son.

"Now children, no busting each other's balls today. We've all made mistakes, right?" She looked over at me, as if she were blaming me for something.

I didn't get it. Why was this on me? I didn't question my feelings for Drew! I wasn't going on dates with my ex. Just then, Drew walked by, chugging a beer as he stared Danny down.

"Grandma, come meet Tilly!" Ben yelled, grabbing Leslie away from us.

"Look, you think I like seeing you like this?" Danny asked.

"Like what? Do I look that awful?" I wondered.

"Honestly? You look miserable. You look like you don't want to be here."

I sighed, "I'm not a good actress, Danny. I'm not a good phony."

He smiled, "That's one of the things I always loved about you."

I smacked his chest, "Why do you have to say things like that?"

"Cami, it's okay if I love you. It's even okay if you love me. We both know *we* will never be again. We have an incredible little boy together, and nothing will change that. But you're my family above everything, and I can't bear to see you like this. I also can't bear to see Drew, as much as I have a hard time with the two of you, I can't stand to see that kid hurting."

"Don't call him a kid," I said, almost in tears. "You make me feel like a cradle robber."

Danny laughed, "He's going to be a dad now. Do you know how happy that news will make him?"

"I want him to choose me, not feel obligated."

"He already chose you, Cami."

I stared at him. Everyone else seemed to be so sure of Drew's love for me, and I was questioning it. Maybe I was the problem after all.

Before I could process it, Chuck Ashton was in front of us, a drink in hand in true Chuck fashion.

"So pleased to see you two kids are back together," he said, in that slithery, belittling Chuck way.

Danny chuckled, "Have another drink, Chuck."

He walked toward the kitchen and I could have killed him for leaving me alone with Chuck.

"Don't you think my son gets tired of seeing you flirting with your ex constantly?"

"Chuck, Drew knows nothing is going on—"

"I was never one to keep up with celebrity gossip," he interrupted me. "But my son and a certain redhead have been plastered across *Razz* Magazine this past month. They made sure not to leave you out... you and Danny look practically inseparable on tour. So tell me, should I still expect my wedding invitation in the mail?"

I had been good about ignoring the tabloids, knowing there was bound to be fudged exposes on my relationship with Drew.

I felt an arm wrap around me in the next instant.

"Can I get you something?" he asked, looking at me.

Drew was trying to rescue me, knowing his father usually said something to hurt me. I was good about not letting him get to me.

"I'm starving," I said.

"Come on, Haley has some appetizers in the dining room."

I walked away with Drew, my hand in his. As soon as we got to the dining room, I stopped and pulled him back. I reached up and kissed his lips lightly.

He smiled at me.

"I love you no matter what," I told him before going to walk past him.

He pulled me back and leaned down to kiss me, but I gave him my cheek instead. He looked hurt.

"You didn't sleep with her?"

He shook his head, "I slept on her couch. She did everything in her power to seduce me, but I couldn't do that to you, Cami. I hope you believe me."

His big, brown eyes were pleading with me and I knew he was telling the truth. I guess I knew it all along, but I didn't want to be that foolish girl who believed a man all because she didn't want to be alone. The difference was, I could be alone. I could survive alone; I did that for years. I didn't want to just survive, though, and definitely not without Drew. I knew he was not the type of man who would look me in the eye and lie to me. His eyes were too deep, too revealing for anything like that.

All I could do was nod my head and rest it against his shoulder. I was exhausted from all that we've been through.

"Danny lectured me."

I looked up at him and laughed, "About?"

"About being stupid like he was. He told me not to let you go... like I had any intention on it."

"No matter what *Razz* Magazine is writing about Danny and me... I can't live without him," I admitted.

Drew released me and looked like I had crushed him.

"He's my best friend, but you're my soulmate. I need you, Drew," I stared into his eyes, feeling incredibly vulnerable.

At the same time, it felt like a burden had been lifted—admitting I needed another person; realizing it was okay to place my heart in Drew's hands. I knew he wouldn't hurt me intentionally. Drew smiled—that big, easy, gorgeous smile of his, and pulled me back into him.

"I love you and I can accept Danny in your life."

I wrapped my arms around his neck.

"Does that mean I have to accept Katie?"

He laughed and shook his head, "Definitely not. Katie and I are two totally different people. I'm not that kid who fell for her anymore. I like my women a little more mature," he winked.

I smacked his chest and he laughed.

"Kiss me," I said.

He flashed another enormous smile before leaning down and bringing his lips to mine. I parted my lips and his tongue slowly massaged mine. I wanted more, but just then, my stomach growled and we both laughed.

We had the room to ourselves for a few minutes as we ate and stole kisses. Everyone else slowly trickled in as their appetites picked up.

Haley came over and kissed mine and Drew's cheeks, seeing the difference in us. Jordan laughed at her before wrapping an arm around her and pecking her lips.

"My wife, the worrier," he teased her.

"Hey, you were worried, too," Haley pouted at him.

"Well, yeah, my brother and my sister were at odds. We need to keep this family together, if not for us, then for the children," Jordan said. "You know, Ben and Biscuit."

I laughed and bit my bottom lip as I thought of the baby inside of me. I looked up at Danny, who was making a plate of finger foods for Ben. He winked at me and I mouthed, "thank you" to him, knowing whatever he said to Drew in the kitchen was important for him to hear.

I glanced over at Haley.

"Can I help you in the kitchen?" I asked.

"Sure," she said.

I followed behind her and when we got to the kitchen, I pulled her into a hug.

"Thank you."

"For?"

"Yelling at me. I needed it."

She laughed, "Cami, you have to know by now that you are loved."

I nodded, "I don't make it easy."

Haley shrugged and laughed again.

"I can't believe Danny was talking to Drew about you!"

"You were present for that?" I asked, wide-eyed. "I want details!"

She nodded and laughed, leaning over the island to tell me the good stuff.

"Danny wanted Drew to know that he had no intention of pursuing you and that you didn't lead him on in any way. He also apologized for telling you he still has feelings for you. He said it was a dick move," Haley continued.

"Danny apologizing to Drew about me?" I gasped.

It was shocking since Danny always acted like he claimed me as his first, and that no guy—let alone someone he considered a brother—should be able to have me.

Haley nodded, "And get this, he gave Drew his blessing to marry you."

My eyes widened, not expecting it all to have went that far. Maybe I wasn't the only one who has grown in relationships. Maybe my ex-husband learned some things as well; like what it means to love someone enough to want them happy, even if it doesn't work in your favor.

"Wow, I can't believe Danny DeSano swallowed his pride and... are we sure he hasn't smoked something today?" I asked.

Haley rolled her eyes, "Give him some credit, he's been cleaning up his act lately."

I laughed, "I know. I'm just kidding."

"Danny even told Drew to blame him for all of your insecurities in relationships."

I shrugged my shoulders, "I can't keep blaming Danny. All I know is I'm a lucky girl, and whatever issues Drew and I have—we'll work it out."

Haley grinned happily and just then, Aylin walked in.

"Mom, do we have anymore hummus? Rad practically inhaled it," Aylin laughed.

"In the fridge," Haley answered.

"So, what's the deal, A?"

"What deal?" Aylin said from inside the refrigerator.

"You told me you didn't feel anything romantic for Rad."

Aylin turned around with a large container of hummus and closed the refrigerator door.

She shrugged, "I'm not sure what I feel yet."

With that, Aylin walked out of the kitchen and I looked at Haley. I was still surprised after my conversation with Aylin that she was still spending time with Rad. She was young and entitled to not take my advice, though. I just hope she doesn't get hurt in the process of trying to please the unpleasable Rad Trick, even if I do like the effect she has on him.

"How do you and Jordan feel about Rad?" I snickered.

She sighed, "He's not my favorite, but from what I can tell, he's a good friend, or whatever they are, to Aylin. I just don't see his appeal. He's arrogant and wears skinny jeans falling off his butt. He has so many tattoos and seems as shallow as a puddle."

I laughed, "I wonder if your parents saw Jordan that way at first."

Haley shook her head, "Jordan never wore skinny jeans."

We both cracked up and just then Jordan walked into the kitchen.

"What's so funny?"

"I was just wondering if you own a pair of skinny jeans?" I asked, and Haley scowled at me.

"No, I don't need tight pants to accentuate my package," he said, kissing Haley's neck.

I rolled my eyes, "He definitely has the arrogant part down."

Haley nodded, but she seemed to get lost in the kisses he was placing on her neck.

"Ugh, how can you guys still be this way? You're an old, married couple!" I yelled disgusted over their display, but also finding it admirable.

Jordan stopped kissing Haley and laughed.

"We're not hung up on age like some people," he said, leaning toward me.

I scowled, "I'm not hung up on age. I just don't make out with Drew in the middle of a party."

"Right," Haley laughed. "You two think you're so slick. I catch you making out all the time!"

"When?" I yelled.

Drew and I weren't prudish in our affections, but we definitely concealed our making out in public more than Haley and Jordan. We stole kisses when we thought no one was watching, but always wound up getting caught because we weren't very good at keeping those kisses brief.

"Um, I saw you guys like fifteen minutes ago in my dining room!" Haley roared in laughter.

"We were keeping people out to give you privacy, but we were all getting hungry," Jordan added.

I smirked and shrugged, "Whatever. We had some making up to do."

Dinner was served a couple of hours later. Haley made a Tofurky roast and Jordan had ordered an already made turkey. Nothing was really homemade this year due to the travel schedule being so close to the holiday. Usually, Haley cooked up a vegetarian feast. I always contributed with a pasta dish, keeping mine and Danny's Italian holiday traditions in.

After dinner, most of us were exhausted, especially the band. They hadn't had much time to adjust from travel. They needed a few days of rest, and so did I— preferably with Drew and my son by my side, along with Biscuit, of course.

Chapter Thirteen

My eyes fluttered open and instead of Drew's face next to mine, it was Biscuit's. As soon as my eyes focused, he was licking me and I could hear his whip-like tail beating the bed—or rather beating Drew as he slept next to us. I heard Drew groan as the tail whipped against his stomach vigorously.

I laughed, "It was your idea to let him sleep with us."

Drew rolled onto his side and ran his hand across Biscuit's short fur.

"I think you secretly love him sleeping with you."

Biscuit maneuvered himself in order to rest his head against my belly and I smiled before looking over at Drew.

"Maybe."

He grinned and Ben stirred from in between Drew and Biscuit.

"We're going to need a bigger bed if we keep this up," I laughed, but also thinking about the baby Drew still had no idea about.

Ben rubbed his eyes and cuddled against Biscuit sleepily. He was too excited about Biscuit and seeing Drew to go to his own bed, so I allowed him to sleep with us too. Drew wrapped his arms around all three of us. I ran my fingers through his hair and wanted to tell him right then about our baby, but there was so much we had to discuss still.

We all lay there snuggling until Biscuit hopped off the bed to scratch at the door. I groaned, not wanting to get up.

"I'll walk him," Drew offered, kissing my cheek and getting out of bed.

Ben looked up at me a moment later.

"Morning Benvenuto," I smiled, leaning down and kissing his forehead.

"Morning Mama," he said, with a huge smile on.

I loved that he called me "Mama" ninety-percent of the time. It was what I always called my mother.

"Did you sleep well?"

"Biscuit snores too much," he pouted.

I frowned, "That may have been me."

"Mom!" Ben put his hand over his eyes.

"What? I can't help it," I said, tickling him.

Biscuit very well may snore, but Drew teases me about my snoring issue all of the time—so I can't be sure who was responsible for disturbing Ben.

Ben and I got up a few minutes later. I looked through the cabinets for something to feed him. I needed to go grocery shopping, but managed to find some oatmeal. Drew came back inside with Biscuit just as the teakettle whistle blew.

"Do you want some oatmeal?" I asked.

"Sure," he smiled, letting Biscuit off the leash and headed over to Ben who was sitting on a stool, coloring on a piece of paper.

Drew mussed with Ben's hair before his eyes went to some paperwork I had on the counter.

"What's all this?" he asked.

I poked my head over the papers and pushed my hair behind my ears.

"One of the many things I need to fill you in on," I smiled.

I stirred Ben's oatmeal and placed the bowl in front of him.

"Careful, it's very hot."

"Okay, Mama," Ben said, going back to coloring.

I finished making mine and Drew's oatmeal and placed the bowls on the breakfast bar.

"Thanks," Drew said, absently reading the paperwork, looking perplexed.

"You want a drink?" I asked, holding up tea bags.

"Just water," he shook his head.

I put a glass under the water filter in the refrigerator before I poured what was left in the teakettle into a mug over a green tea bag. I handed Drew his water and sat down next to him.

"Benny boy, eat please."

Ben took a spoonful and blew on it before licking the oatmeal off.

"Good?" I asked.

"Yes," Ben said, but I knew instant didn't live up to what Drew usually made us.

His oatmeal was steel cut oats with real fruit, nuts, brown sugar, maple syrup and a dash of cinnamon. He always made it to perfection. Compared to the artificially sweetened instant Quaker Oats I was serving, it was a five-star meal.

"So, what does this all mean exactly?" Drew asked, looking up at me.

I mushed around my oatmeal and smiled at him.

"Colin will basically be running Out of the Woods."

Drew's mouth dropped, "But you love your job. You're a work-a-holic."

I took his hand in mine and shrugged.

"I love you and Ben," I said, just as Biscuit let out a cry as if he truly wanted some oatmeal. I laughed, "And Biscuit."

"You can love us all without quitting your job."

"I'm not quitting," I rolled my eyes. "I own the damn company. I get final say still. I just don't have to be there all the time or on tours or at awards shows if I don't want to be."

Drew stared at me blankly, "But you *want* to be part of those things."

"I did, yes," I agreed. "Don't get me wrong, I'll still want to be part of those things from time to time, especially since Tortured is part of my family. I like being around them, but I want to be a full-time mother and... whatever I am to you," I said quietly.

Drew leaned over and kissed me deeply.

"Are you sure this is what *you* want? Because I'll be fine with whatever you want."

"I've been thinking about what I want, and I'm tired of this need to be working all of the time. I missed out on so much time with my mother because she had to work. I don't have to work, I made sure of that at a young age; that I could provide for my family, but I am not a slave to work anymore. My business runs just fine without me."

Drew flashed me his dimples, and I would take him to bed if Ben weren't in the room.

"That's because you're sexy and brilliant."

I bit my bottom lip and kissed him, "Sexy is your opinion and brilliant is debatable. I'm dumb enough to think my son would actually eat this crap," I laughed, nodding over to Ben.

He was spoon-feeding the oatmeal to Biscuit, and missing terribly. The poor dog had oats on his nose that he was trying to lick off. Drew laughed and took a heaping scoop of the oatmeal and ate it.

"It's delicious," he shrugged.

I rolled my eyes and took a small spoonful. Not long after I swallowed it, I had to run to the bathroom.

"Cami, really? It's not that bad," he laughed.

A couple of hours later, Drew and I were walking through Central Park with Biscuit on a leash, and Ben holding my hand. It was a perfect fall day. There wouldn't be many of these days left this season. The brutal New York winter was just around the corner. When we got to a leash-free area, Drew bent down to let Biscuit free. I stopped him.

"I'm worried."

Although Biscuit has adjusted to us well, I didn't know how he would be with other dogs and in an open space.

"What if he runs away?"

Drew smiled at me, "I don't think he's going anywhere. Neither am I," he said, pecking my lips before proceeding to let Biscuit free.

Ben took off running with the dog, finding a stick. He tossed it, and like a natural, Biscuit charged after it and brought it back to Ben like it was something they'd been doing for years.

"He must have had a family before," Drew said. "He's a natural with the kid."

I took his hand in mine.

"The shelter said he was a street dog, abandoned as a puppy. A homeless man reported him, saying he was trying to latch onto him."

Drew thought for a moment.

"I guess he wanted a family."

I nodded, "He reminds me of us."

Drew laughed and put his arm around me, "Oh yeah?"

While I definitely had abandonment issues, so did Drew. His mother was almost nonexistent in his life while his father wasn't much of a father—more of that asshole friend you're unsure of why you've kept around because he's not much of a friend at all.

"Yeah," I smiled at Drew. "Wanting a family, but being turned away. He looks tough, but he's a mush inside."

Drew smiled and took a glance at Ben and Biscuit before giving me his full attention.

"I am so proud of you for making the decision about your company," he said, staring into my eyes. "If it's really want you want and no one else."

I nodded, "It really is what I want. I feel liberated by making this decision. And I want to work on that whole therapy thing, too. I'm sorry I was being so stubborn and rude about it."

Drew reached out and rubbed my cheek, "I understand and I'm not thrilled about therapy either, but I think it's something that would help us. At least we'll be going through it together."

I nodded and laced my fingers with his, pulling our hands against my chest. Drew leaned down and kissed me. I heard a couple of snaps go off and peered over my shoulder to see some college-age guys taking photos of us on their camera phone. Drew looked over at them and they pretended like they weren't watching. He sighed and looked back at me.

"I'm not ready to retire yet."

I looked at him funny, "Okay. Good. You're only thirty-two."

"I know I said I wouldn't mind retiring early, but I love the game and I thought... I figured it would come to a point where I would have to choose. Or after the injury, I feared it wouldn't even be my choice, but I'm glad I still have one," he said, relieved.

"Drew, I'm not Katie, remember? Just like you never made me choose between work and you, I would never do that to you either. I love that you're a Yankee—even with inappropriate comedians calling me your ball girl and strangers snapping our picture for Instagram," I laughed. "As long as I have you."

Drew laughed, "I still want to kick that guy's ass for making that joke at the VMAs."

I shrugged and rolled my eyes.

"I guess I figured with you taking time off work, you'd want me to also," Drew said, delicately.

I smiled, "I think you have a few championship rings to earn first. Besides, I wouldn't mind being a player's wife for a while. You know, sit in the stands and gossip with the other wives and girlfriends," I teased.

He knew I hated that.

Drew laughed and wrapped me close to him, kissing my forehead. Biscuit ran by with the stick and Drew ran to catch up with him, grabbing the small branch and tossing it. Biscuit charged after it, and Drew scooped Ben up, placing him on his shoulders before he stomped around with him. I watched on, admiring my growing family.

That night, Leslie took Ben home with her to Staten Island. Since he had been on the road with Danny and me, she felt overdue for Grandma time with him.

The guys of Tortured wanted to go out to Carney's, which wasn't uncommon while we were all home. Drew didn't always come, sometimes because he was away, but most of the time, it was due to Danny giving him the cold shoulder. It was the band's hang out and Drew didn't want to ruin that for them.

He agreed to go that night, though. As much as I was happy he was coming along, I felt uncomfortable about it. With all that's happened, me admitting to Drew that I kissed Danny, along with all of the tabloid speculation, as well as Danny's hurt feelings by my relationship with Drew, it may never be comfortable between the three of us. I couldn't expect that the conversation Danny and Drew had on Thanksgiving would change any of that.

Drew was taking extra-long to get ready, and I was in a t-shirt and jeans. I put on the most minimal amount of make-up and tossed my hair into a low side ponytail. It was just Carney's, after all.

When Drew finally came down the hall, I expected him to have full make-up and a gown on, but he was dressed casually—no make-up or gown, thankfully.

"Did the oatmeal make you sick too?" I wondered with a laugh.

"No," he shook his head. "I guess I'm just moving slowly. Ben wore me out at the park."

Granted, my son was a handful, and Drew hadn't been playing ball everyday anymore, but still, he worked out daily. I didn't buy that he was tired—unless he was emotionally. I know I definitely was!

"Are you going to have energy for me tonight?" I asked, running my hand across his ass, and squeezing.

He smirked and winked, "I always have energy for you."

We took a taxi to Midtown where Carney's was. Jordan, Haley, Sebastian and Tasha were already there. Greetings were exchanged and Jordan asked if we wanted drinks.

"Beer," Drew said, as his eyes glanced up at the football game on.

"Cami?"

"I'm not in the mood to drink," I said, hoping no one would insist.

I suppose I could get a glass of wine, but I rather not. The waitress came over and smiled at us. Not only were we regulars, but famous regulars. We always had good service and we always tipped well.

"What can I get you guys?" The bubblegum cracking twenty-something asked.

She was just Darren and Danny's type—speaking of, they walked in at that moment.

"Can we get two pitchers of beer?" Jordan asked. "A round of tequila shots and a Shirley Temple for these two ladies," he pointed at Haley and me, teasingly.

I chuckled and shrugged, giving into the children's beverage he ordered for me.

"You can make mine dirty," Haley chimed in and Jordan laughed at her.

Haley much rather have a sweet nonalcoholic drink, but she liked being one of the guys when we were at Carney's—the first time she ever got drunk was there, but she rarely had more than two drinks when we went out. It only took a little more than that to get her wasted.

"Anything else?" The waitress asked.

"Barbeque wings and nachos, please," I ordered.

Usually that was what Danny got. The table would pick at it, but he practically polished off everything by himself.

"And an extra side of celery and carrots," Haley added.

"You bring down our unhealthy average," Sebastian chided her, and we all laughed.

Danny and Darren made it over to us.

"Who's the new girl?" Darren asked, eyeing the waitress as she took another table's order.

"Too young, bro," Danny patted his back.

"Screw that, she's legal. Cami can date babies, why can't we?" Darren asked, knowing I'd be pissed.

"You can put my shot directly up Darren's ass," I said, giving him the finger.

Everyone laughed and Drew put his arm around me, pulling me in close to kiss my temple.

"My cougar."

I elbowed him and he winced as I caught him in the ribs harder than I intended to. I immediately rubbed the spot and flashed him a playful, but apologetic smile. He pouted at me and I kissed his lips.

Darren sat down next to Sebastian while Danny took the seat between Drew and Haley. Talk about awkward.

"Ben told me all about the park," Danny said. "He's so happy to have a dog," he finished with a smile.

I grinned, "Yeah, now he has a way to hide food he doesn't want to eat."

Danny laughed, "Stick to Italian, Cam. Let Drew take care of the rest."

I stuck my tongue out at him.

"So are we on for the gym tomorrow?" Drew asked.

I wondered if I heard him right.

"Yeah, what time?" Danny responded.

Drew looked at me, and contemplated a time for a moment.

"How about two?" Drew asked. "Cam, you want to come with us?"

"Huh?" I asked, dumbly. "Excuse me?"

Drew and Danny shared an amused look between them.

"The gym tomorrow?" Danny asked.

"You? Me? All of us?" I stammered, completely confused.

"You used to work out with me once in a while," Danny reminded me.

"And we haven't hit the gym together in a while..." Drew added.

I looked over at Haley who was listening in and she shrugged.

"I'm in the twilight zone."

"All right, forget her," Drew laughed. "Just the boys then. J, you want to come?"

I was still dumbfounded and decided I didn't want to be part of this gym outing. It was normal for both Danny and Drew to keep a gym regimen, but it wasn't something they had done together—with or without Jordan—since before Drew and I got together.

The waitress returned with the drinks. I took a sip of my Shirley Temple and gave Drew the cherries. I hated them, but he loved them. He tied the stem into a knot with his tongue and winked at me as he showed me. I laughed and leaned over to whisper to him.

"Should I be jealous of you and Danny?"

"I have my other brother back," he smiled.

He looked sweet and innocent in that moment, not the hot short stop with the skilled, cherry-stem tying tongue. Drew took a gulp of beer before excusing himself to the bathroom.

I leaned over to Danny.

"Thank you."

"For?"

"Making Drew happy."

Danny laughed, "I think that's you—not me."

I shrugged and took another sip of my drink. The food came and I dug into the wings like nobody's business. I was keeping up with Danny. We both reached for the last one and he laughed.

"You can have it."

"Are you sure?"

"I'll order more," he said, and I grabbed the last wing, devouring it.

Drew came back to the table and stared at the empty basket of wings.

"D, shit, that must be a record. Thanks for saving one for me," Drew laughed.

I was sucking barbeque sauce off my fingers when Drew looked over at me. He looked at my plate and laughed seeing half of the chicken bones on my plate.

"Hungry, baby?"

Someone got over the microphone to announce karaoke would be beginning. I groaned.

"Ugh, I thought Thursday was karaoke night?"

We hardly ever went to Carney's on a Thursday. We needed to protect our ears. Besides, everyone wanted Tortured to sing then, and sometimes, they just wanted to be spectators—not celebrities.

"They must have moved it to tonight since they missed it for Thanksgiving," Tasha shrugged.

Another order of wings later and two more pitchers of beer, we were immersed in bad singing of Bon Jovi, Frank Sinatra, and Britney Spears songs. We were still having a good time, though, enjoying the drunken slurs from the performers.

"We have a special performer tonight. Our very own Yankees short stop, Andrew Ashton!"

I shook my head and looked over at Drew. He winked at me before standing up. He loved to make a fool of himself. It wouldn't be the first time he had gotten up to sing karaoke or dance on a random bar or stage. Drew loved to entertain. I couldn't dislike him for it, even if he occasionally enjoyed trying to pull me into the mix and embarrass me.

Sound Wave's "Home" came on and I shook my head with a blush. This was *our* song. He was definitely trying to pull me into this.

"Aww," Jordan and Haley teased together.

I rolled my eyes and raised my glass up to Drew from the back of the bar as he began to sing. Sebastian pulled out his phone and began taking a video.

I'm not perfect

My heart's got, got a permanent defect

But your love, the one thing I can't reject

I know, like me, pain is what you expect

Time to let go, ohh

You made me dream, yeah
When I've given up on things
Please love me for who I am

In spite of everything
I've ever done
Because you, you are everything
I always wanted
And never thought I would find

Baby, you take me home
When I've got no place to turn
You pick me up
When I am dropped so far down
And on my own
Baby, you take me home
You're the safety net
That'll catch me when the day is done
I want to go home with you
Baby, take me

I think Drew may have been slightly drunk. His voice sounded shaky and as the chorus kicked in, he started to go into the crowd like he was a boy band member. He was caressing girls' cheeks and giving guys high-fives. He was the epitome of cheese! This side of him only made me love him more, but if some other guy was up there doing what he was doing, I'd probably gag.

Drew took the cordless microphone with him as he made his way to the back of the bar, where we were sitting. Oh God. He began singing the chorus to Haley first, and then Tasha before booty-bumping the waitress as she went by. I thought the waitress was going to pass out.

Drew had the entire bar with their cell phones out, taking photos, or video, and wanted to get close to him—men and women. This performance surely would be all over the internet within minutes.

Just as the second verse began, Drew dramatically slid onto his knees in front of me. He was singing to me and I wanted to hide, or kiss him, but mostly, I just laughed. His voice wasn't great, but it wasn't too painful either. A bit off-key here and there. He and Jordan definitely did not share the family musical genes.

As Drew sang, he would clutch my hand and stroke my face theatrically, and I still felt a cross between wanting to run away and taking him right there.

> *I stare at your face*
> *And I know what I was missing*
> *Hell baby, I've got scars*
> *And you needed space*
> *We both needed time, time, time*

To find this magic place
Baby, you take me

You take me home
When I've got no place to turn
You pick me up
When I am dropped so far down
And on my own
Baby, you take me home
You're the safety net
That'll catch me when the day is done
I want to go home with you
Baby, take me

With you, I'm alive
With you, I see truth
Behind every lie I felt inside
I am home, home, home
With you, I am home[†]

Drew finished the song, and the entire place gave him a standing ovation as he buried his face into my knees. I wondered if he was embarrassed, which didn't seem like him, or going to pass out. Maybe he had more alcohol than I had realized. I probably should have saved some wings for him to soak up the beer.

"Drew? You okay?" I asked, leaning down.

Just then, he popped his head up and was holding out a gorgeous, light blue diamond ring tucked inside a velvet box. My mouth dropped and I couldn't process what was happening.

"Cami, will you marry me?"

I couldn't comprehend the question. I had already asked Drew to marry me months ago, but it didn't quite feel official with all of the problems we'd been having, and because, while Drew wore his diamond-encrusted band, I had no ring showing we were engaged. At least not yet...

I smiled stupidly at him.

"Remember who asked first."

Drew laughed, "Is that a yes?"

"Yes," I said, pressing my forehead against his. "A thousand yeses."

"I saw this ring and it reminded me of your eyes," he said, kissing my lips as he slipped the ring on.

[†] The lyrics to "Home" were also written and owned by Sandy Lo.

I had forgotten where we were and who we were with for a moment, until Drew lifted the microphone to his lips.

"She said yes!"

Everyone at Carney's went crazy and Drew stood up, pulling me into his arms and kissing me again. I looked at him and couldn't hold it in anymore. I stretched up and got close to his ear.

"I have an engagement present for you," I said.

Drew smiled, his dimples showing. "I think that's something for later."

I laughed and nodded, "It'll be here in about seven months."

Drew's smile fell, unsure of what to make of my comment. To help confirm it, I unwrapped his arms from around me and placed both hands on my belly.

"I'm pregnant," I said.

Drew looked down between us and then at my face before he threw an arm in the air and shouted, as if the Yankees just won the World Series. I laughed as he picked me up again, this time, grabbing my legs to wrap them around his waist. He held me effortlessly as he continued to cheer, and the crowd around us was going nuts! I'm relieved he was carrying me, or else I might have been trampled on by the rally of bar patrons around us.

"She's having my baby!" Drew yelled, and he didn't need the microphone for everyone to hear him.

As if Tortured won an award, or come to think of it, they'd react the same way if the Yanks won the World Series as well, the members of the band jumped up and began congratulating us. Drew placed me down, but grabbed my hand, as if he didn't want to lose physical contact with me.

Danny patted Drew on the back before they paused and hugged. He then pulled me into a hug and I gave him the biggest smile. For a split second I let my smile fade, not sure how Danny really felt about celebrating this moment with Drew and me. I knew that was his problem, not mine, though. When Danny smiled and looked into my eyes, I knew he was genuinely happy for us. He would be okay, and he was welcoming Drew back into his life to prove it.

Jordan pulled Drew into a hug next.

"I'm going to be an uncle again!" he yelled, kissing my cheek.

It took a long time for the night to settle down, but when it did, I welcomed the silence as we entered our apartment building.

"I heard the news," Gary said. "Congratulations Miss Cami and Mr. Drew."

We smiled and thanked him before getting into the elevator.

"Good news spreads even quicker than bad news," Drew said. "I always thought that was the other way around?"

I shrugged, "Maybe times are changing."

He pulled me into a kiss, as he unzipped my coat. I began to work on the buttons of his coat as well. As soon as we got into the apartment, Biscuit wanted attention. We greeted him briefly before locking him out of the bedroom for the first time.

As soon as we began making love, we could hear the whimpers coming from outside of the door and we both laughed.

"Poor baby," Drew said.

"See, we spoiled him," I said, pulling Drew down for a kiss.

"Maybe we should let him in," he said, drawing a lazy circle around my nipple.

"Uh uh, I can't have sex while Biscuit is watching," I objected, as I physically shivered over Drew's touch.

He laughed and got off of me, taking me by surprise.

"Drew!" I yelled. "Do not let Biscuit—"

It was too late. Drew opened the door and Biscuit bounded into the room and jumped onto the bed. I put my hand to my forehead, and tried to cover up with the comforter. I felt I needed to protect Biscuit, and all of his doggy innocence from what Drew and I were about to do.

"Now what? We're just supposed to do it with him next to us?"

"No, come on," he motioned for me to follow.

Where my naked fiancé wants me to follow, I go. We headed to the guest bedroom and closed the door, picking up right where we left off.

After making love, we held each other and I stared at my engagement ring. Drew looked at me and smiled.

"Do you like it?"

"I love it," I said wrapping my arm around him.

"I was really kind of nervous tonight," he admitted.

I smiled, "You did great, even if your goal was to embarrass me."

He laughed, "That wasn't my goal. I just—I wanted as many people to know how I feel about you."

I kissed him and pressed my forehead against his.

"Thank you for overcoming your fear of proposing."

"It should have been me proposing in the first place," he sighed. "I was chicken shit."

"Are you really intimidated by me?" I asked, still wondering if that was true, or a problem for us.

He laughed, "Of course I am."

I propped my head up and looked at him seriously.

"I'm intimidated by the strong person you are. I'm intimidated by how hard you work, how hard you fight. I'm intimidated because I have never loved anyone like I love you, and that is pretty scary, you know?"

Gone was all of Drew's playfulness. He was serious and I could tell he was scared.

"I don't want to lose you, Cam, and I came so close..."

His voice got caught in his throat. I quickly sat up and pulled him into a hug. I pushed him back against the pillows and lay on top of him. I held myself up by my arms and stared into his eyes.

"It is scary," I said, allowing my tears to fall. "I'm intimidated by you, too, you know? You're so full of life and love, and I'm not always like that... I didn't want to bring you down, or not give you what you needed—"

He interrupted me, "Cami, you give me everything I need and more. I'm sorry that I was reliving my past. I was just worried about our future. You were so worried about the idea of us making a baby, I thought maybe you didn't want one—with me."

I shook my head in disbelief.

"Drew, why wouldn't I want to have your baby? It was just so much pressure and I knew how hard it would be..." I said as he reached up to wipe my tears before I couldn't hold myself up anymore.

I fell down to his chest and he wrapped his arms around me.

"I'm sorry."

"Me too," I whispered before he rolled me over.

Drew began kissing my face before working his way down to my neck, and in between my breasts. He stopped at my belly and kissed it. He just laid his head there and I ran my fingers through his hair, knowing he was having a moment with our baby, though he couldn't feel anything. I am pretty sure we fell asleep just like that.

Epilogue

"Mama! Mama! Mama!" Ben yelled from somewhere in the house.

"Ben, Ben, Ben!" I shouted back as he came running out to me.

"Biscuit took my shoe!"

I put my hands on my hips and looked at my son questionably.

"Did you throw your shoe toward Biscuit?"

I knew the dog well enough now that he didn't take things unless he witnessed you throwing it. The game was on then.

"Um, maybe?" Ben said, smiling innocently.

"Biscuit!" I yelled, and the dog came running, his nails sliding against the wood floor in our penthouse.

"Drop it," I said to the dog, and Biscuit immediately let go of Ben's shoe, which now had a little drool on it, but otherwise, was in perfect condition. "Here you go. Are you finished packing?"

"Almost."

Ben was spending a few weeks on the road with Tortured. It killed me to be away from him for so long, but I was in no condition to travel. I was eight months pregnant and though everything was going well, I was ready to give birth. I was uncomfortable and hot constantly. Don't get me started on Drew—when he was on the road, he called and texted neurotically. He would even have little minions checking up on me. All I wanted was some alone time to binge watch *Veronica Mars* and *The Walking Dead*, but every minute someone was calling or showing up at my door. Haley, Jordan, Danny, Aylin, Cisco's wife, and even Topaz!

I'm still not sure how Drew tolerates her friendship, especially now that Will Nostri and she have officially called it off. Drew's a much better person than me, but I will admit, underneath her celebrity image, Topaz is just a small town girl who had big dreams, and cares about her friends and family. She's actually really thoughtful and compassionate toward animals. She loves to walk Biscuit for me.

Gary called and said I had visitors. A few of us were going to the Yankees game together. A few moments later, Danny and

Jordan walked in. Ben and Biscuit both came running down the hall. Ben had on his Yankees hat and #12 jersey. Danny scooped him up.

"Daddy, I'm all packed for the tour!"

Originally Ben didn't want to leave me. He wanted to be around when the baby was born, but I assured him he would be back by then. If I happened to go into labor early, Danny promised he would get Ben home as quickly as possible.

"Good job, buddy," Danny high-fived Ben. "Are we ready to go?" he asked, looking over at me as I tried to get off the couch.

"Mama is so slow," Ben sighed.

"Hey!" I yelled as they all laughed.

Jordan reached his hand out to help me up. We took a car to the Bronx and when we got to our seats, all of the players' wives made a big deal about how I looked "ready to burst". Ugh, do they think that makes me feel better? I just hoped I'd be able to get my figure back in time for my wedding in the fall. I found a dress I loved, but it was mermaid-style. Tasha and Haley forced me to get it, and I might live to regret it.

Just as the game began, Topaz showed up.

"Hi Tami—argh, Cami. I'm sorry," she scolded herself. "I got used to you being Tami. You should have told me that wasn't your name sooner."

"I did," I grumbled, but she was already greeting everyone else.

I hope Will was okay with Topaz still showing up to games, but then again, there wasn't much he could do about it. Topaz's grandfather owned the team. She plopped herself down, in her four inch heels and hot pink dress right next to Danny. Immediately, his eyes went to her long legs and I rolled my eyes. This was going to be sickening.

The game started, and I tried to focus on it instead of my discomfort in my seat. Jordan kept looking over at me, and then at Danny and Topaz.

"Is this bothering you?"

"What?" I asked.

He motioned toward my right. I waved it off.

"Whatever," I laughed, but then felt a tightening in my belly.

I rubbed my hand across where the pain was and Jordan looked concerned.

"Cam?"

"I'm fine. The baby must be in a weird position."

Drew ended the inning catching the last out. It was time for the seventh inning stretch. I got a text message from Drew.

How are my babies?

Uncomfortable. I wish they had a couch up here or something.

I'll add that to the suggestion box. ;-)

Thanks. Great catch by the way. This game is in the bag.

By the top of the ninth inning, I had quite a few different feelings in my belly. Jordan kept looking over at me and I waved him off. I knew what was happening. I could recognize contractions when I felt them. I also knew it could take hours before I gave birth. I didn't want anyone to panic, especially not Drew. After the game was over, I planned to casually tell Jordan and Danny what was going on. I would then calmly call Drew and tell him he needed to hurry up with press interviews so we could go to the hospital.

By the end of the ninth inning, though, I was breathing pretty heavy and holding my stomach.

"Cami, are you going into labor?" Jordan demanded.

I blew out a breath of air and nodded.

"Shit," Danny said, overhearing and breaking away from flirting with Topaz.

Jordan and Danny stood up before I could get a word out.

"Guys," I tried to stop them, but they were lifting me out of my seat.

"I'll call Drew," Jordan said, knowing he had been keeping his cell phone on him in case of anything with the baby and me.

"No," I whined. "He's up at bat next."

"Really Cami?" Danny laughed. "I think this is more important."

"But we're so close to beating the Red Sox," I argued, through the breathing.

"The baby's coming?" Ben asked, jumping up excitedly.

"We're going," Jordan demanded as he placed his phone against his ear.

Just then, Drew was announced to the plate.

"Hey Drew, Cami's in labor," Jordan said.

I was confused. I looked back to the field to see Drew at the plate with his phone to his ear.

"Are you kidding me?" I laughed incredulously before yelling toward Jordan's phone. "Drew, hit one for your little girl!"

Jordan rolled his eyes, "Yeah, Cami wants to wait until the game's over. She's crazy."

Jordan hung up a second later. I looked at him expectantly and he shrugged. The next thing I knew, I heard the crack of the bat. I turned back to the game and sure enough, Drew hit the loudest homerun I had ever heard. The bat was broken and he rounded the bases faster than I had ever seen anyone run. The Yankees won! Drew took off straight to the dugout, and Jordan and Danny continued hauling me out of the players' box. Ben ran to my side and held my hand the entire way to the parking garage.

There was a lot of movement around me, and it was too much for me to take. I had an entire entourage following me to Danny's car. A few of the players' wives along with Topaz were following behind. I couldn't process what anyone was saying to me. I just wanted Drew to be with me, but at least Ben was holding onto me protectively. By this point, paparazzi had caught on to what was going on, and were blinding me with flashes. I could hear Jordan and Danny arguing with one photographer, who was blocking the way to the car.

"Can everyone just back the fuck away?" I yelled, which seemed to at least silence everyone, but they weren't going away.

Ben looked up at me, "Mama!"

"Sorry Ben," I apologized before getting into the car and reaching out to him.

Danny lifted him into my arms and I instructed him to get into his car seat. The commotion started up again and I was grateful it was due to Drew's arrival. He didn't say a word to anyone. He sprinted to the other passenger side door and hopped in. Ben was between us, but Drew leaned over and kissed my forehead.

"Sorry," he apologized.

"For what?" I asked, wincing from another contraction.

"All of this, and being late?" he asked, placing a hand over my belly.

"Don't worry, Drew," Ben patted his arm. "The baby is still in Mama's belly!"

I laughed and Drew kissed Ben's head.

"That's good news, buddy."

"I'm glad you got to finish the game," I said, as Jordan and Danny were getting in the car.

"This nut didn't want to interrupt the game!" Jordan shook his head.

I shrugged, "I didn't see a need to rush. I was just thankful there were no extra innings."

Drew laughed and I placed my hand over his on my belly. Danny took off toward the nearest hospital. I was kind of mad I wouldn't get to deliver the baby with my own doctor, but the contractions were getting closer together. Besides, it was hard enough making it through traffic in the Bronx. Manhattan would be ten times worse.

I had to have a cesarean birth, which I knew already. Drew was fairly calm. Danny was a mess when Ben was being delivered, but Drew was making jokes and I had never seen him look so happy.

His eyes brightened when he heard the first cry and I was so thankful I could give him this gift that was so important to him. I couldn't get a decent look at my little girl, but soon, she was in Drew's arms and then was placed on my chest. She was gorgeous—I could even see dimples in her cheeks already, just like her daddy!

I didn't last much longer than that. I remember Drew kissing my forehead before I knocked out. Hours later, I was awake and ready to get to know my baby better. Drew was holding her when I woke up. The nurse told me he hadn't put her down yet.

"We still have to pick a name," I said, as he placed the baby in my arms.

She opened her eyes and they were blue, darker than Ben's and mine, which made me wonder if they'd stay blue. Maybe she would have her father's brown eyes instead.

"I know," Drew sighed, sitting on the edge of the bed.

We hadn't come up with any name we liked. I hoped when we looked at this little girl, something would pop up, but all I wanted to call her was "sweet pea" or "pretty girl", because that's what she was.

"Maybe we should let Ben name her like he did with Biscuit," Drew laughed.

"He'll name her Spot or something," I giggled.

"Probably," Drew shrugged and looked down at our child. "I love her so much already."

He looked into my eyes and then looked down at the baby. I ran my fingers through his hair.

"I hope she's just like you."

Drew looked at me and shook his head.

"I want her to be like you."

I laughed and turned my head, thinking he was ridiculous. He lightly pulled my chin toward him. He leaned down and kissed me softly.

"I love you. You've made all of my dreams come true."

I smiled and moved into kiss him deeper as I stroked the five o'clock shadow on his face.

"I love you too. The dream is only beginning. You have us for the rest of your life."

Drew smiled big when we parted from another kiss.

"Dream! What about Dreamer?" Drew asked.

"Dreamer what?" I furrowed my eyebrows as his excitement made the baby stir.

I rocked her slightly and Drew rubbed her dark-haired head.

"Dreamer Ashton-Woods," he smiled.

I looked at him surprised. We had agreed on a hyphenated last name, thinking our names sounded good together, but only in that particular order. But I had never heard of Dreamer as a first name before. It sounded something hippy-like; something Haley would name her child.

"Dreamer?" I questioned.

"Yeah," he smiled. "She's our dream come true and I want her to be a dreamer, like us," he winked.

I smiled, "You are adorable and super cheesy."

We both looked down at our daughter.

"Welcome to the world, Dreamer," I said, leaning down and kissing her forehead.

Drew reached over and held my hand as my eyes closed. I had this overwhelming sense of feeling whole. I had everything I could ever want and need.

Acknowledgments

Thank you to my editor Melissa Marini. I hope you're not too mad at Cami and Drew anymore, haha. To the readers of this series, I hope you feel that these characters have become a family to you like they have for me. To my family and friends for always supporting me. To my Mom up in Heaven who somehow gives little nuggets of inspiration to me when I'm feeling lost. I sometimes feel like your presence is with me as I write, which is why I always adds bits of you.

About the Author

Sandy Lo is an author, blogger, journalist, and brand manager. Always a self-starter, Sandy founded StarShine Magazine at only 18! While pursuing her journalism career, she wrote contemporary romance stories as a hobby until 2009 when she decided to self-publish her debut novel, "Lost In You". In 2010, Sandy released "Dream Catchers", the first book in the rock star romance series of the same name. To date, there are seven books in the "Dream Catchers" series with an eighth book in the works. Other notable works include "The Watch Dog", "Indigo Waters", and "Decaf For The Dead".

Sandy has been included in the "50 Writers You Should Be Reading" list by The Authors Show, and "Dream Catchers", "Breaking The Moon" and "Indigo Waters" reached the Top 100 Best Selling Coming of Age novels in Amazon's Kindle Store while "The Watch Dog" reached the Top 10 Ghost Stories on Amazon.

As a journalist, Sandy was the first person ever to professionally interview Taylor Swift and has received personal endorsements for her books from members of boy bands Backstreet Boys and 98 Degrees. She is also one half of the blogging duo, All's Fair In Love & Writing with her partner, Steven A. Clubb.

Sandy also added screenwriter and producer to her credits when she got the opportunity to work on the indie horror film, "Reed's Point".

When she's not writing, reading, or working, Sandy enjoys traveling, dancing, movies, cooking, and spending time with her boyfriend, bunny, and other loved ones.

For more information on Sandy Lo & her projects:

Check out other titles in the "Dream Catchers Series" by Sandy Lo on Amazon!

Dream Catchers – Book 1
Breaking The Moon – Book 2
Expressions – Book 3
Take Me Home – Book 4
The Reunion – Book 5
Spotlight – Book 6
Fanning The Fame – Book 7

And look out for these stand-alone novels also available on Amazon!

Lost In You
The Watch Dog
Indigo Waters
Decaf for the Dead

Sneak Peek:

Spotlight

Dream Catchers Series – Book 6

Available Now on Amazon

Prologue

True love was something I knew existed, but I also believed it to be rare. Relationships crumbled too often for me to think it common.

My parents said the words "I love you" often—to me, to one another, to their friends. But I hadn't given any thought to what those words meant. I loved lots of things, like animals, other children, ice cream, and my family. Outside of that, I never had a dire need for any particular person or object growing up, until recently.

I know how much I love my parents, but the kind of love Mom and Dad have for one another is what really baffled me. They embody true love. In today's world, you don't see it often, but it was always right in front of my face.

Throughout my school years, I couldn't remember a single friend whose parents weren't divorced. While traveling with my dad's rock band, Tortured, I would meet so many celebrities who were on their second or third marriage. Some never settled down with anyone at all.

Even my dad's best friend, Danny and the band's manager, Cami, who were married almost as long as my parents had been, got a divorce a few years ago! I came to find out Danny was cheating on Cami, and they never had what she would describe as true love to begin with. The demise of their marriage opened my eyes to the fact that love is sometimes (most of the time) a novelty that wears off.

I used to be content surrounded by two loving, amazing parents who had the coolest careers. Mom is a notable photographer whose work had been featured in just about every magazine across the world. Dad, AKA Jordan Walsh, famous lead singer of Tortured, is renowned for his voice, songwriting, good-looks and humble personality. I'm proud of who my parents are and all they have accomplished.

While people think they're cool for their professional accomplishments, I find their love for one another to be the most significant thing about them. They're incredibly in sync with each other. They've been together for over twenty years and they still act like teenagers with a crush. I want that.

I don't know when I will have it—if I will ever have it. While I am grateful for the life I've been blessed with, relating to my peers, making friends and having boyfriends is difficult.

I am around the band more than anyone else and they're all at least twice my age. When I am not on tour with Tortured, I am accompanying Mom on photo shoots with teen heartthrobs, or cheering on Uncle Drew, shortstop for the New York Yankees, at home games. That is normal for me, but it isn't for the average person.

Now that I'm no longer a teenager, I have grown tired of tagging along with my parents. I used to be a boisterous free spirit who went with the flow and didn't stop to think about anything but the moment I was in. Senior year of high school was a serious wake-up call. I grew frustrated with my so-called friends when they continuously wanted to use me to get to Tortured or the Yankees or set them up with a celebrity.

Kayla was the closest I had to a best friend. We met when we were fourteen, and kept in touch through social media and text messages while I traveled with my parents. She'd always beg me to Face Time from backstage at whatever event I was at and made lots of ridiculous requests—like celebrity phone numbers.

I used to be happy and excited about life. When I turned eighteen, I suddenly felt alone. I couldn't trust any of the friends I made in high school and meeting new people was not easy.

I keep waiting for something and I don't know what that something is. I thought college would be better. I could discover some kind of career calling and find real friends, but ultimately, I want to find true love—to have a partner in life to express these emotions to. I don't want to feel used for my last name, the celebrity company I keep, or my money.

I'd settle for a simple crush on someone my own age who wasn't super out-of-reach. The hugest crush I ever had was on my dad's hot tour manager, Colin Houlihan. As soon as he said hello to me with that adorable Irish accent, I was planning our life together at eight-years-old.

Not long after I became infatuated with Colin, I asked Mom how she knew Dad was her soul mate. I hoped her explanation would help me identify the feeling within myself one day.

"Did you know right away?"

She laughed, "No, I hated your father at first sight."

My eyes widened, "Hated him?"

She nodded, "I thought he was gorgeous, of course, in that unpolished way he has about him, but we were totally different people. I feared boys, especially ones that smoked and had tattoos..."

"Dad smoked?" I gasped, disgusted.

"Yes, repulsive, right?" She rolled her eyes and then

laughed, as if she was lost in the memory of when they first met.

"So, did Dad fall for you right away?" I wondered. "Did he annoy you so much until you just went out with him?"

Fame or no fame, Dad had a way about him. He was good at getting people to do what he wanted, especially girls. He was what most people called charming, and I've been told many times that I have inherited his charm. I don't know about all of that since most people were too entranced with my father than to ever notice me.

Mom laughed at me thinking Dad forced himself on her.

"Your father thought I was a stuck-up brat. But we both felt like we had to prove something to the other one. I think we came off so different that we were both a little intrigued, and secretly liked challenging each other," Mom shrugged. "We got to know each other and realized you shouldn't judge a book by its cover," she concluded.

She looked at me the way she did when she wanted me to come away from something with a lesson. *Never judge a book by its cover*, got it, Mom. She didn't realize the response I was searching for, though.

I never did get a clear answer of the moment Mom knew Dad was her true love, or how she knew. Does the feeling just hit you? Was it gradual?

Now at twenty-one, I feel I should know something about relationships and love, but I am still clueless and desperately wanting to mature in that department. As for the whole "don't judge a book by its cover" … well, I never did, and sometimes I think I should have. Sometimes a book turns out exactly like its cover, and its one you never should have read to begin with.

Chapter One

"Aylin, you don't have to decide your major right now," my college advisor chuckled at me.

I am a sophomore at NYU and really want to figure out my career. I took a couple of semesters off to travel with my parents and be a nanny for my Aunt Cami and Uncle Drew. I thought it would give me time to figure out my life path.

My parents tell me I'm in too much of a rush to grow up, and maybe I am. I was surrounded by grown-ups my entire life. They were past this whole indecisive, career-choosing, love-seeking phase. I hate not knowing my future. I want answers. I want to know who I will be and who I will be with. I've always been a tad impulsive and impatient. Okay, maybe I am more than a tad of both those things.

"Mr. Vecchio," I sighed. "I feel like I'll just delay the time I'm spending in college. I mean, what if I decide to be a doctor and I haven't taken any courses related to that?"

I ran my hand through my blonde hair and Mr. Vecchio looked at me, obviously amused. He has a graying goatee with one hair too long that seems to tickle his upper lip when he talks. It must bother him because he scratches the goatee every so often. I contemplated grabbing the pair of scissors on his desk and snipping it off for the past ten minutes.

"Do you want to be a doctor?"

"No way," I shook my head, trying not to focus on the goatee. "Too much blood and pain and politics."

I know doctors help people, but the medical industry is riddled with corruption and medication that cures shit—and by shit, I mean not much of anything.

"I'm more of a holistic type."

"So, you want to study holistic medicine?" Mr. Vecchio asked, crossing his hands, and placing them on the desk, with a mocking expression.

I shook my head, "No, I don't want to go into medicine at all."

He was totally missing my point!

"Aylin, are you wasting my time today?"

I pushed my hair behind my ears and groaned.

"You're my guidance counselor. Help guide me!"

He rolled his eyes, "You're a kid still. Go out and join a sorority. Stop worrying so much about your career. It'll come to you. Make friends, date, party a little and next semester, we'll talk."

He stood up and made his way to the door cueing me to leave. I looked at him in disbelief.

"Join a sorority? Party a little? *That* is your guidance?"

Mr. Vecchio chuckled again, which really must have made his goatee tickle his lips. Immediately, he ran a hand over his mouth before giving me a condescending look.

"You need to lighten up, kid."

Ugh, I hated people who called me kid!

"Why am I even in college then? I'll just go party," I shrugged, standing up, grabbing my bag, and storming out of his office.

Okay, maybe I was a little high-strung lately, but I wasn't always that way. I did whatever anyone else wanted to do, or wanted me to do.

Aylin, you want to come on tour with us instead of going to your prom? Sure, Dad.

Aylin, can you get us tickets to a Yankee game? Sure, friends who don't give a damn about me.

Aylin, can we have sex? Sure, Rad.

Ugh, Rad Trick. Maybe he had a little more to do with my irritable, "help me, I'm lost" state than I'd like to admit. He was someone I thought was my friend. I should have known any guy with a name like Rad would be trouble. I was warned, too—by my parents and Cami—that Rad's bad boy image in the tabloids wasn't all publicity.

Rad Trick is a solo artist, who likes to think of himself as a rock star, but is more pop-rock that would be played on the Disney Channel in between those over-acted cheesy shows that I indulged in way more than I like to admit.

He is tall, kind of skinny with thick, dark hair, almost black eyes, and olive skin.

His parents are from Greece and his full first name is Radamus.

He is managed by Out of The Woods Entertainment, my aunt Cami's company, which also manages my dad's band, Tortured. I had met Rad a bunch of times in passing, but he asked me to lunch a while back and we began hanging out whenever he was in town.

I knew Rad's image was tarnished. I knew about the stints in rehab and how frustrated Cami always seemed when talking about him. Like my mother taught me, though, I didn't judge books by their cover.

Rad didn't want to get to know me because I was Jordan Walsh's daughter or Drew Ashton's niece. That was a first for me. I felt special. Rad truly seemed interested in who I was as a person.

We listened to each other when it felt like no one else understood. He told me about his addictions. I told him about my inexperience with love. He talked about how strict his parents were. I told him how laid back mine were. We shared the same feelings toward our friends—that they were using us.

One thing we didn't share was a mutual attraction. Sure, I thought Rad was good-looking, but I didn't feel drawn to him in any physical way. I wanted to be, though. Wouldn't that have made life easier? If I could just force myself to fall for someone who genuinely liked me? I enjoyed talking to Rad, though. He told me I was a good influence on him, and I believed him. It made me feel good about myself.

He also said something about my parents one night after too much alcohol—on my part—that struck a chord. I had never thought about it before, but it made me wonder.

"Your parents are a little selfish, huh?" he asked, as we sat in his Upper West Side penthouse on a super uncomfortable, modern couch.

"Selfish?" I gasped. "No," I shook my head vehemently. "They're great. They've given me everything I need and more. I'm lucky," I smiled, but felt a twinge in my stomach of uncertainty.

Rad flashed a smile as he reached out and brushed my cheek. He always found little ways of touching me. I knew he wanted more with me, but I was grateful he hadn't made a move... yet. I hoped I would return his affections eventually.

"It's okay, Aylin. It doesn't make them bad people. They both have busy careers and they did what worked for them, to keep you all together. But did it work for you?"

"Did what work for me?"

The alcohol and Rad's accusations along with how close we were sitting were mixing me up.

"Traveling around the world? Being pulled out of school? Living in their shadow?"

I pulled back from him, "I'm going to go."

Rad grabbed my hand and pulled me down.

"I'm sorry if I upset you."

I looked at him and didn't realize I was crying until he brushed back my tears. He pulled me into a hug and I couldn't stop the tears from falling as he consoled me. When I finally looked at him, he made his move. He kissed me and I felt too overcome with emotions and confusion to do anything but kiss him back.

It was a nice kiss, but I didn't feel any more for him than I had before it happened. I politely left and walked around aimlessly. I never spoke about my parents' "selfishness" again.

Rad took that moment, and the vulnerability it evoked within me, and tried to recreate it whenever we were alone, which I tried to keep to a minimum. I missed our talks, but I was afraid of facing his affection and exposing anymore negative feelings.

Of course, I didn't take Cami's advice and try to cut off the friendship.

"It is impossible to get over someone you see all the time," she explained when I told her about Rad's one-sided attraction.

Cami knew that better than anyone. From what I understood, she harbored a crush on my dad for twenty years! I'm glad she and Uncle Drew are getting married in a week; they're perfect together.

Instead of listening to Cami, I continued to hang out with Rad. I even began initiating kisses with him. Why? Out of fear of losing the only real friend I had, and still hoping he would grow on me romantically, like Mom and Dad grew on each other.

One night Rad and I were making out—after too much alcohol again—and I was feeling turned on. It wasn't necessarily an attraction, but my hormones took over. I had never even been to third base before and wanted to wait to find love, but I felt strongly for Rad as a friend. I had rather lose my virginity to him than any other guy in my life at that moment. I didn't stop him when he put his hand up my dress and into my panties.

He pulled his hand away right when I was about to go over the edge and looked into my eyes.

"Can we move into the bedroom?"

I knew this was a grown-up decision. It could change everything. But right then, I wasn't thinking clearly. Rad had worked me up just enough that I wanted to finish what we started. I wanted to become a woman; one who made decisions for herself and didn't drift aimlessly and comfortably like I always had.

The walk of shame I took at three a.m. had me feeling awful. I felt bad for leaving, but I thought it would be worse if I stayed. Sneaking into my Riverside Drive brownstone made me feel even worse, like I did something wrong. Why did it feel wrong? I was twenty-one! I don't have to ask permission to have sex or stay out late.

My dog, Tilly, came running to me and I pet her quickly, hoping the sound of her clicking paws on the wood floors didn't wake Mom. Dad was somewhere in England on tour. I was grateful I wouldn't have to look into his eyes for the next few days. Could fathers tell when their daughter's innocence was gone? Although, I still felt pretty damn naive and like a little girl more than ever. It was a stupid move. It wasn't a sign of maturity or taking control. I was anything but in control.

As I got changed for bed, I thought about Rad and wondered if I could ever love him, or even like him enough to date. That was why it felt so wrong; I knew he had feelings for me and they were not reciprocated. I cried myself to sleep with Tilly by my side.

Tilly had only been in my life for a year, but she was the best dog. Dad and I rescued her from an ASPCA event I was volunteering at. Mom was skeptical about having to take care of a dog with all the traveling we did, but it's worked out.

The next morning, I worried what I would say to Rad or how he would feel about me sneaking out on him. He sent me a text that afternoon, but it wasn't what I expected to see.

Had a great time last night. Thanks ;-)

I guess I expected something along the lines of him asking why I left or that awkward "we need to talk" text. For the next few days, I kept waiting for something like that to come, but it never did. I didn't receive any other communication from him until almost a week later. The text came in at night. Late at night.

Wanna come over? :-)~

Ok

It became clear to me I was a booty call. Maybe that's all I ever was to Rad; a conquest.

That whole situation along with the need to find out who *I* am and what *I* want had me all sorts of screwy.

When I got home from school, the irritation from visiting with my guidance counselor and receiving a follow-up text from Rad had consumed me. This time, Rad's text said something about missing my body and it made me cringe. I slammed down my bag and noisily searched through the freezer for vegan ice cream. Mom and I weren't complete vegans, but just about.

I found the ice cream wedged in the back of the freezer covered by giant bags of frozen broccoli. We kept an emergency stash in case of PMS or particularly bad days. Today wasn't an awful day and it was a little early for PMS, but after my "best" friend reduced me to friends with benefits and my guidance counselor told me to join a sorority, ice cream was called for.

I sat down on the couch with the carton of Turtle Trails and a spoon while flipping the Yankees game on. I glanced at my phone to see Rad sent me another text.

Are you ignoring me? I'm leaving tomorrow for L.A. I really want to see you before I go.

I shoveled a huge scoop of ice cream into my face before picking up my phone and responding.

Okay. Not at your place. We need to talk.

I have a meeting at Out of The Woods in a few. Want to meet me there and we can go to Serendipity?

I looked at the ice cream in my hand and knew a Frrrozen Hot Chocolate was not what I needed. I got sick the last time I had one. Serendipity and pizza were my two huge dairy exceptions, and I always paid for them later.

Sure. What time?

The T.V. announced Uncle Drew to the plate and I gave the game my attention for a moment. Tilly jumped up on the couch beside me and I welcomed her warmth as opposed to the cold container in my hands. I heard the front door open and Mom giggling on the phone with someone. She walked into the living room, holding a dress bag.

"I can't wait to see Ben give you away. It's going to be so cute," Mom cooed.

It was obvious she was talking to Cami. Mom was almost as excited for the wedding as Uncle Drew and Cami were. If you knew Cami, you'd know getting excited and giddy about something didn't always go hand-in-hand for her. That kind of changed when she and Uncle Drew began dating.

"Hey A," Mom called to me.

I waved at her with the spoon in my hand and she must have figured out what kind of day I was having.

"Cami, I'll talk to you later," she said draping her dress over the arm chair just as the T.V. roared.

Uncle Drew hit a homerun. Before Mom could hang up, I could hear Cami cheer through the phone. She was obviously watching the game too, and I had to laugh. Mom sat on the other side of Tilly who acknowledged her with a wag of her tail.

"Emergency stash?" She asked, motioning to the carton and I nodded. "Bad day at school?"

"My guidance counselor is a jackass."

"Aylin," she smirked.

Mom secretly enjoyed when I cussed. She once told me I was adorable when I was mad, which frustrated me since I was trying to be serious—not adorable.

"Mom, he told me I need to lighten up and party more," I sighed, handing her the ice cream.

She laughed and took a heaping scoop of Turtle Trails.

"What? I don't think he's supposed to advise that," she said with her mouth full.

"Right?" I huffed.

"Forget him. How about we go out to dinner and make fun of his misshaped goatee?"

I laughed. I love my mom. Rad wasn't my best friend. Mom is.

"I wish I could. I'm meeting Rad," I said glumly.

"Oh," she nodded.

She sounded disappointed and I wanted to tell her what's been going on. I told my parents everything, but I didn't want to upset them. I didn't want to prove everyone right about Rad and reveal my stupidity.

"I love you, Mom," I stood up.

She smiled, "I love you too. Are you okay?"

I shrugged, "I just want to find my place, you know?"

She tilted her head, "You're right where you belong."

Leave it to Mom to say something cheesy and perfect. It made me angry that Rad called my parents selfish when they care so much.

"You know what I mean," I said. "I want to figure out my career and find my peeps."

She laughed, "Your peeps?'

"I love you guys, but I don't have friends—"

"Aylin, you have a ton of friends," Mom said. "Everyone loves you."

I sighed, "Mom, you know that I stopped hanging out with people from high school."

"That was your choice, A."

"Yeah, well, they just didn't seem like good friends when they would ask for tickets to a Yankees game or concert all the freaking time. I mean, you saw how those girls would gawk at Dad when they'd come over."

Mom stood up and pulled me into a hug.

"They're kids and even adults are so wrapped up in putting celebrities on pedestals. Your dad hates it. That doesn't mean they didn't like you. Do you think if you were some stuck-up snob that they'd still be your friend even with the perks?"

I pulled away and looked at her. Mom's grey eyes were determined to convince me my friends cared about me.

"Yes, I do."

She didn't know how to respond.

"Maybe your guidance counselor is right. You need to party a bit and make some new friends."

I rolled my eyes and pushed her lightly.

"Right, like you were such a party animal in college," I stuck my tongue out at her.

"You don't want to be like me," she laughed. "I had social claustrophobia! It was awful."

"Being like you isn't so bad, you know?" I smiled.

Mom shoved me this time and we laughed.

"You'll find your way," she said, as if she could promise that to me.

I nodded, wanting to believe her.

Chapter Two

I took the Subway to West 57th Street. While I loved New York and the convenience of public transportation, I wish I had the opportunity to drive more. Driving in Manhattan could be a huge inconvenience. There was more stopping than going and parking was a whole other story. Uncle Drew bought me a sweet eco-friendly car for my 16th birthday, much to my dad's dismay, and I rarely drive it. I want to take a road trip over winter break; that would be the best medicine to get me out of the funk I was in.

I arrived at the Out of the Woods office and had to sign-in at the lobby.

"Who are you here to see?"

"Rad Trick," I said, not thinking much about it.

The shiny bald male security guard looked at me skeptically. He must have thought I was a fan. When Cami came into the office daily, I didn't have these problems. I would pick Ben up at her office so often that all the security guards and doormen recognized me. Baldy was obviously new, and I wasn't around nearly as much as I used to be.

"I'm sorry, but we can't let fans up to see Mr. Trick."

"Oh no, I'm his friend..." I laughed, but the guy wasn't buying it.

He gave me a deadpan stare.

"Are you visiting anyone that actually works here?"

"Fine, I'm here to see Colin Houlihan," I smacked my hand on the desk with a shrug.

Again, I received the deadpan stare. Thankfully, he picked up the phone and I prayed he wasn't secretly calling the cops on me.

"I have an Aylin Ashton here to see Colin Houlihan," he said, looking at the I.D. I had given him before glaring back up at me.

I smiled mockingly.

"Oh, I see," he said. "Thank you."

He hung up the phone and deadpanned yet again.

"Mr. Houlihan stepped out."

I blinked at him a few times and sighed.

"Fine," I grabbed my cell phone and was about to tell Rad I'd meet him at Serendipity.

I didn't know why he wanted to meet at the office anyway. Not that I minded. I enjoyed coming to the office to see all the fast-talking managers charging around. If I was truly honest, coming to the Out of the Woods office meant I would get to see Colin. And he was the ultimate reason I loved coming here.

I turned around and took a few steps away from the desk to text Rad my issue. Just then, Colin walked into the building holding a large drink tumbler and a paper bag in his hands.

"Aylin," he flashed that gorgeous smile of his.

Colin had such a charm about him. He had the broadest shoulders and always wore buttoned up collared shirts with rolled up sleeves. I've never seen him completely dressed down, but at the same time, he made the business look appear casual.

He had bright green eyes with a hint of blue to them—different than the green that was in my hazel eyes with the "flecks of gold" that my mother always liked to point out. *Just like your father*, she'd coo.

The thing I loved most about Colin, though, was his smile. He had these perfectly straight, white teeth and thin lips that curled up when he talked. He had defined laugh lines around his mouth that seemed to complete him. His smile took over his entire face. It was genuine. He laughed a lot and smiled often, and I loved that.

In an office full of balls-to-the-wall type of people, Colin didn't seem anything like that. You would never pin him to be tough or ruthless, but he was; he just took a different approach with people.

He won Cami over enough for her to make him the Chief Operating Officer of the company, which shocked us all—including Colin! He was one of the youngest COO's in the world, at only thirty-two.

"Hey Colin," I said, relieved to see him.
I wasn't simply relieved, though. I was downright excited to see him, and trying hard to act casual about it. He walked up to me and haphazardly hugged me with his drink and food in hand. I wrapped my arms around his slender, but toned torso and felt

like a little girl. Granted, it didn't take much to make me feel short at only 5'2, but Colin was over 6 foot tall!

"Are you meeting Rad here?" he asked, his Irish accent making me take a moment to figure out that he said the word "here".

"Yeah, is that okay?"

"Of course. I'm sad you're not here to visit me, but..." he shrugged.

I felt the blush take over my face as I pushed my hair behind my ears; a terrible nervous tick I had that I desperately tried to be conscious of, but failed to prevent ninety-nine percent of the time. Colin walked me back over to the desk with his arm around my shoulders.

"She's with me, George, thanks," he held his hand up.

"Oh, okay, sir," Baldy AKA George said, giving me one last stare.

I stuck my tongue out at him and he laughed, finally. Colin and I walked toward the elevator.

"Made a new friend, I see?" he winked before pushing the button. I shrugged my shoulders and laughed.

The elevator came down and we stepped onto it.

"How's school going?"

"Fine."

"Just fine?"

I looked over at him, "I'm bored. I'm thinking of finding a job to spice up life."

He laughed, "Your life isn't spicy enough?"

I stopped watching the floors climb and realized I sounded like a whiny brat.

"My life is great. I mean, what other twenty-one-year-old can say she's been to the Grammys multiple times, traveled the world, ran the bases at Yankee Stadium, and still managed to get into NYU?"

The elevator dinged and we stepped off.

"Not to mention," Colin added. "Was featured on the cover of People Magazine and is dating," he said before gasping. "The amazing Rad Trick."

He was teasing me, but I wasn't amused as I followed him down the hall.

"I had no choice in that whole People Magazine thing. I was like seven," I rolled my eyes. "And I'm not dating Rad."

"Does he know that?" Colin asked, holding the office door open for me.

I flashed him a look.

"Lighten up, Aylin. You're still young. It's okay to be confused," he put a hand on my shoulder.

I hated that he called me young—like he really meant to call me a kid. I hated that he seemed to understand what I was feeling. Mostly, I hated what I was feeling. It felt like resentment, and I didn't want to resent anyone or anything in my fortunate life.

"There's the hottest blonde I know," I heard and Colin mumbled something incoherent; something not nice and not directed at me. I wish I had caught exactly what it was.

J.J. Fowler was coming at me and before I could react, he hugged me. His large hands squeezed me against him so tight that I had to use my body strength to break away.

J.J. works at Out of the Woods and directly handles Rad. He is also Rad's best friend and all around douchebag. He is the epitome of creepy music manager; somewhat good-looking, but slimy. He's in his mid-twenties and arrogant as hell, but his close-knit relationship with Rad kept him employed.

"Be nice," Colin shoulder bumped J.J. as he passed him. He turned around and looked at me. "Hang in there, A," he winked.

I smiled at him, and wanted him to come back. J.J. put his arm around me.

"How's it going?"

"Fine. Where's Rad?"

"He's talking with his new tour mate. Are you going to visit us?"

Because that's really what I wanted to do; go on another tour other than my father's. At the same time, I hated when I didn't travel often. I loved being home, but became bored—probably due to the lack of friends around. That road trip I've been thinking about was much more appealing than visiting Rad on tour. Being surrounded by fans, paparazzi, roadies, and insane schedules was not the kind of road trip I wanted.

"No." I said.

As J.J. spoke, we walked further into the office. A few assistants said hello to me. I knew one of them, and the rest of them knew me. It was weird when that happened. I didn't have to introduce myself to most people who paid attention to celebrity news. Random people on the street would shout to me, "Hey Aylin!" I'd be polite and wave, but it was awkward.

Sometimes I wondered if I would follow in my father's musical footsteps had it not been for the attention from strangers. I love playing guitar and dabbled in songwriting. I didn't know if that was something I wanted to pursue or keep as a hobby. I had a knack for drawing and creative writing, too, but again, I didn't know if I wanted to make a career out of it. Mom offered to employ me at her company, Moon Halo Photography & Design, which was named after me; Aylin means moon halo in Turkish. While I enjoyed drawing, graphic design made me want to break my computer.

It all seemed overwhelming to make these big life decisions at my age. How will I know what I want to do in twenty years? What I'm feeling now could be fleeting—God, I hope it was fleeting. I needed to escape life for a bit, but with midterms and Uncle Drew and Cami's wedding coming up, I was stuck drowning in school and celebrity attention for a while.

Giggling filled the office followed by Rad's raspy voice. He was causing the high-pitched fit of giggles from a girl. He reveled in those reactions.

"Hey Aylin," Rad smirked, as if he was trying to stick it to me by flirting with the cute, innocent redhead by his side.

J.J.'s arm slid off my shoulder and brushed across my ass. I snapped my head at him and shoved him.

"Relax, it was an accident," he laughed.

I didn't trust him and I really didn't like him.

"Hi, I'm Aylin Ashton," I said, sticking my hand out.

"I know," the girl said with a bright smile. "Your dad is so hot. I had his poster on my wall."

"I'm sure he'd be happy to hear that."

I laughed inwardly. My dad would hate to hear that! As much as my father was at ease performing in front of crowds, he wasn't really into the celebrity that came along with it, which is why I can't resent him even if I wanted to. We're kind of in the same boat. Just because he wants to share his art with the world, does not mean he signed his life way. People forget that.

Dad was never okay with being a poster on someone's wall. To him, that was a teen heartthrob thing. That was a sellout thing. He couldn't control how or how much Tortured blew up though. I was proud to be his daughter. Sometimes I should remind myself of that when I'm feeling like I don't exist outside of him.

"You don't have my poster on your wall?" Rad asked her, pretending to be offended.

He probably was being serious. He's as cocky as they come, which is partly why I was never attracted to him.

"Well, um, yeah, of course," the girl lied.

"You're a music artist too?" I asked.

"Oh yeah, duh, I'm Julie Hart. My first single comes out next week," she laughed, realizing she didn't introduce herself.

"I discovered Julie playing in this cafe across the street," J.J. chimed in.

"Cool," I smiled.

"Are you girls hungry?"

I looked at Rad and then at Julie.

"Starved," she grinned at him like a schoolgirl.

She might be a schoolgirl actually. She looked sixteen.

"I've got to do some work. You guys have fun," J.J. said, flashing me a sly smile.

It was obvious J.J. knew I slept with Rad, and I just hoped his big mouth didn't blurt things like that out to Cami, or Colin, or worse, my father.

"Rad, can I talk to you for a minute?"

"Sure, what's up?"

"I mean, alone. Sorry Julie."

"No worries," she shrugged. "I'm going to look at the pictures on the wall again. I can't believe I'm being managed by Cami Woods' company," she squeaked before walking off.

I nodded over to one of the conference rooms, hoping Colin wouldn't mind, and closed the door.

"I told you I wanted to talk. What's with you inviting Julie?"

"Oh, I figured we could hang with her for a bit and then," he said, stepping closer to me and wrapping his arms around me. "You and I can have a proper goodbye."

He smirked as his lips moved closer to me. I pushed him away.

"You're unbelievable," I sighed. "I'm not your booty call."

"No, of course not," he laughed. "We're friends," he shrugged before stepping closer. "...with benefits."

I shook my head, "No, we are not. That night was a mistake, Rad. I was... I don't know what I was thinking."

"You weren't thinking. You were finally listening to your body," he said, reaching out and running a hand down my neck.

I pushed him away.

"Rad, I love our friendship and I don't want to ruin it. I want things to go back to the way they were."

He laughed, "Right Aylin. Do you think I was ever interested in being your friend?"

I glared at him.

"I've wanted you in my bed since I met you. I thought I made that clear. I get you made me wait, being a virgin and all. Now that we broke the seal, what's the big deal? I'm not looking for love, so it's cool if you don't have feelings for me or whatever. But you wanted me too," he said, and I finally saw the Rad Trick everyone warned me about.

I couldn't help myself and shoved him hard enough for him to hit the wall. He shoved me right back, and I seriously wanted to hit him.

"Stupid kid, that's what you are," he shook his head at me.

"Right back at you," I said before storming out of the conference room.

I tried to hurry past everyone without making a scene. Rad was right; I was stupid to ever believe we could be friends or that he cared about me in any way.

"Aylin," someone pulled my hand.

"I have to go," I said, not looking up at Colin.

"Hold on," he said. "It's been a bit. Let's catch up."

I looked up at him and forced a smile. I knew he could see through the fake expression on my face; tears were brimming my eyes.

"Please Colin, I need to go."

"Come on, A. You could always talk to me."

He flashed a sexy smirk and I almost hated him for it. Was he referencing the crush I always had on him or was he being genuine? I couldn't decipher between sincerity and phoniness apparently.

History proved Colin to be a terrific shoulder to cry on, ear to listen or someone to brighten a lousy day. He was all those things for me growing up on a tour bus.

"Another time," I pleaded.

I couldn't talk to Colin Houlihan about my sex life. He was there to treat me to ice cream or help pick out a birthday gift for my father, but to listen to me whine about giving up my virginity to sleazy Rad Trick? No way!

"Are you sure?"

I nodded, tucking my hair behind my ear as I looked up at him.

"I'll see you at the wedding."

I left the building as fast as I could, hoping I wouldn't run into anyone else I knew.

Made in the USA
Columbia, SC
15 February 2023